And Then Everything Unraveled

ALSO BY JENNIFER STURMAN

The Pact

The Jinx

The Key

The Hunt

And Then Everything Unraveled

by Jennifer Sturman

Point

Library of Congress Cataloging-in-Publication Data
Sturman, Jennifer.
  And then everything unraveled / Jennifer Sturman. — 1st ed.
    p. cm.
  Summary: Delia's mother is declared dead when her ship disappears on the way to Antarctica,
but when Delia arrives in New York to live with an aunt she has never met, she begins trying to
figure out what really happened to her mother.
  ISBN-13: 978-0-545-08722-3 (alk. paper)
  ISBN-10: 0-545-08722-8 (alk. paper)
  [1. Missing persons—Fiction.   2. Aunts—Fiction.   3. High schools—Fiction.   4. Schools—
Fiction.   5. New York (N.Y.)—Fiction.   6. Mystery and detective stories.]   I. Title.
  PZ7.S94125An 2009
  [Fic]—dc22

                                                                                      2008046958

        12 11 10 9 8 7 6 5 4 3 2 1   9 10 11 12 13 14/0

                                Printed in the U.S.A.
                                First edition, July 2009
                        Book design by Elizabeth B. Parisi

This book is dedicated to Michele Jaffe.

Acknowledgments

Thanks to: Aimee Friedman, Abigail McAden, and the wonderful team at Scholastic; Laura Langlie, my fabulous, non-jinxing agent (though I might've just jinxed that); Michele Jaffe, without whom nobody would know what to wear; Manuel Urrutia, expert on all things Colombian; and various Sturmans, large and small.

And Then Everything Unraveled

One

It's hard to believe, but this whole thing didn't even start until a couple of weeks ago, when my mother left for Antarctica with one of her environmental groups. They were on their way to document the damage to polar ice shelves from global warming, just in case there's still anyone out there who doesn't think it's a problem.

Of course, I didn't know then that my life was about to change forever. Everything seemed completely normal. T.K. — my mother's full name is Temperance Kittredge Truesdale, but for obvious reasons she prefers to go by T.K. — anyhow, she travels a lot, so I was used to her being away. In fact, I was sort of glad about this trip, because it meant I could spend the last days of summer at the beach, guilt-free.

I have a semisecret surfing habit, something neither my mother nor my friends know much about — T.K. because she doesn't believe surfing is a "high-return use of scarce time" and my friends because everyone thinks business plans are cooler than slacker sports in Silicon Valley, where it seems like nearly all of the parents and most of the kids have started their own Internet companies.

Google and Microsoft are already fighting over a widget my best friend, Erin, came up with for mobile messaging, and my other friend Justin sits in on engineering classes at Stanford — for fun, not because anyone makes him. Meanwhile, I do a lot of pretending to understand what they're talking about.

I'm pretty sure they're just as mystified about how I spend my spare time, not that we really discuss it. But my dad was the one who taught me how to surf, and even now there's something about hitting a wave just right that makes me feel like he's still around, and like things make sense in a way they never do on dry land.

All of which is a long way of explaining why I spent the whole afternoon at Ross's Cove that Monday, making the most of nobody paying any attention to what I was up to. I probably stayed out later than I should have, but I had no idea that everything had already begun to unravel.

The big black BMW parked in front of our house was the first clue that something wasn't right. Even without the TJW-4 vanity plate I would've recognized the car. Only Thaddeus J. Wilcox IV would drive something that flashy in our neighborhood, where it's practically illegal to own anything but a hybrid.

Thad's the guy who manages the day-to-day operations of my mother's company. He comes by the house sometimes, but it's always to see T.K. — his being there when she was away was sort of strange. Still, when I saw his car, I just figured he was dropping off some paperwork for when she got back, and mostly I was hoping he'd be gone before I got inside. While Thad's supposed to be a total genius at business, he's not exactly the most gifted conversationalist.

So I was taking as long as I possibly could to hang up my wet suit on the porch when I heard Nora calling my name from the kitchen. Nora's our housekeeper, and she stays overnight when my mother's out of town, which means a lot of TV and junk food since those are two of our shared interests. She also likes to ask about my love life, but that's a pretty short conversation since I don't have one.

I went in through the back door, and Thad was still there, waiting for me in the kitchen with Nora and fiddling with his BlackBerry, which I think must be surgically attached since I've never seen him without it. They sat me down at the kitchen table, and Nora poured me a glass of milk, which she knows perfectly well I hate.

I was so busy protesting about the milk that I didn't even notice the weird look on Nora's face until after she'd taken a deep breath and said, "Delia, honey, we have something important to tell you."

Then Thad cleared his throat and explained about the SOS signal my mother's ship had sent out, and how none of the ships or planes that came to the rescue found a trace either of her ship or any survivors.

"Oh," I said.

"Do you understand what Thad is saying?" Nora asked. Her forehead crinkled, and she automatically reached up a hand to smooth it. Nora's a grandmother, but she's very proud of not looking like it, and also of looking that way naturally. One of our other shared interests is checking out pictures of face-lifts gone horribly wrong on AwfulPlasticSurgery.com. "Sweetie, if the ship went down, and they didn't find any survivors, it means your mom is d —"

"Uh-huh," I said.

They were probably expecting a more over-the-top response. And I have to admit, for a split second I did feel like somebody had vacuumed out my insides.

But almost instantly that feeling gave way to a bizarre sort of calm. When I reached for the emotion that was usually right there, waiting to be tapped, I came up empty.

Because I just couldn't believe my mother was dead.

I still can't. I mean, everyone else is using the past tense when they talk about her, but it's all a huge mistake. It has to be. I don't know what happened exactly, but T.K. will explain everything when she returns.

And I'm sure she will return. This is a woman whose favorite appliance is a label maker — she's way too organized to die by just disappearing like that, and she's much too determined to let a little thing like being stranded in the Antarctic do her in.

Especially when she's the only parent I have left.

My dad, Ashok Navare, and T.K. met in the computer lab at Stanford. I suspect I was conceived there, too, but that's one of those things I'm happier not knowing about. They were in the same graduate program, and together they came up with a way to speed up e-mail traffic on the Internet. This sounds like an easy fix, but whenever people send e-mail, the company my parents started makes money. Only a fraction of a penny each time, but since it happens billions of times a day, it adds up.

T.K. was really into building the business, but my dad cashed out to pursue his true passion, which was, embarrassingly, the type of extreme sports they show on ESPN2. Some fathers play golf, and the ones who're trying extra hard to seem young might do yoga. Ash was the only one jumping out of planes with a surfboard strapped to his feet. He liked defying expectations, and people tend not to expect Indian software engineers to be into that sort of thing.

The irony was that he died doing something as ordinary as grocery shopping. He was coming out of the Whole Foods in Palo Alto when a car swerved to avoid a runaway cart and hit him instead. That was three years ago, and I'd thought I was finally okay with it, but hearing about T.K.'s disappearance made me miss him all over again.

So, I was already down to one parent, and I knew T.K. would never just desert me, and definitely not in such a haphazard manner. And it wasn't like there was even any proof that she was actually dead — I didn't get the science gene, but I'm still enough of my parents' daughter to know how important empirical data is, and in this particular situation there wasn't the tiniest shred of it.

But nobody seemed to agree with me on that point — not Nora, and not even Erin and Justin, though they were a lot nicer about it than people like Thad. And nobody paid the slightest attention to any of my ideas about search-and-rescue missions, either. A person can't be declared officially dead until she's been missing for seven years, but the general consensus of everyone who was old enough to have a say — as in, not me — was that my mother's gone forever. Thad and the lawyers hardly waited seven seconds to dig up T.K.'s will.

Knowing my mother, I wasn't surprised that she had a will or that she'd filed copies in all of the appropriate places, including in a folder labeled WILL in the cabinet in her home office, right behind the folder labeled WETLANDS PRESERVATION and right in front of the one labeled WIND FARM — SOLANO COUNTY. But I was still surprised by what it said.

Her plans for her money were completely predictable. I knew she had a lot and I knew exactly what she'd do with it. Sure enough, a sensibly sized chunk goes to me — enough to cover the basics, but not enough for Paris Hilton to start worrying about the competition. The remainder's supposed to go to organizations supporting "socially liberal but fiscally conservative causes."

Her plans for her company, TrueTech, were predictable, too, since it's been entrusted to Thad's care. There was also some ominous language about Thad training me to take over one day, and he seemed pretty worked up about it, but he's always worked up about something. Since I've barely finished the tenth grade, and since I have plenty of other things to worry about, it seems as if this is a request we can safely ignore for now.

No, the stuff about the money and the company was fine. It was the final paragraph that floored me. Here's what it said:

> *In the event of my death prior to my daughter, Cordelia Navare Truesdale, reaching maturity, I appoint my sister Charity Dennis Truesdale of 15 Laight Street, Manhattan, to act as her legal guardian.*
>
> *However, while Charity will have sole custody of Cordelia, I appoint my other sister, Patience Truesdale-Babbitt of 888 Park Avenue, Manhattan, to act as her trustee, with full discretion over all financial and academic decisions.*

This would have been fine, too. I know orphans are supposed to go live with their relatives, and even if my parents had ever been married, what family my dad had is in India — it wasn't like I expected anyone to send me to an entirely different country.

There was just one small problem: I'd never even met my

mother's sisters. Or anyone else in her family, for that matter. All I really knew was that T.K. hadn't spoken to her parents since before I was born.

The rift started when she decided to go to Stanford. Truesdales had been attending Princeton for generations, so this was a big deal. Then things got worse when she decided to have me on her own. Apparently, voluntary single motherhood wasn't done, at least not in her parents' social circles, but T.K. considers marriage to be an "archaic manifestation of patriarchal oppression" and says life is too short to waste on "antiquated convention and East Coast snobbery."

She'd explained this back when I was in the second grade and wondering why I didn't have a lot of relatives giving me presents on my birthday or coming to watch my soccer games. But when she'd told me about her family, all she'd really said about my aunts was that the three of them didn't have much in common besides being the victims of their parents' unfortunate taste in names.

And, as if finding out that my mother had recklessly handed my future over to two complete strangers wasn't enough of a shock, then came the real kicker. T.K. saw fit to add the following little coda, right before the signatures and dates and notary's seal:

To be clear, I make these arrangements only as a last resort.
For Cordelia's sake, I hope they never become necessary.

These aren't exactly the sort of words in which an orphan can take comfort, even an orphan who's only temporarily an orphan. But they also didn't stop Thad from calling up my aunts and turning my entire life upside down.

After several hurried conversations among the adults on each coast and a lot of me fruitlessly pointing out how ridiculous it was to write T.K. off so soon, Nora packed my things into boxes to be shipped to my aunt Charity's, and Thad arranged for my plane ticket. It was all done so quickly that I barely had time to process what was happening, though I did manage to sneak in a final afternoon at Ross's Cove before saying good-bye to Erin and Justin.

It was the first Sunday in September, right before Labor Day and the start of the school year, when Thad drove me to the airport in San Francisco. Being Thad, he insisted on getting there ridiculously early and then walking me all the way to the security checkpoint. If they'd let him, he probably would've followed me onto the plane to make sure I buckled my seat belt properly, but fortunately he didn't have a boarding pass and I was considered old enough to travel by myself, even if I didn't have any say over where I was going.

Six hours later, I landed in New York.

Two

I was a bit on edge by the time my flight arrived, a little after midnight. It turned out that a long plane ride alone wasn't exactly the best way to take my mind off T.K. calling my aunts "a last resort," and it hadn't helped that the movie was about tap-dancing penguins. I didn't want to think about how they were much better equipped for polar survival than my mother.

So I wasn't feeling like the least anxious version of myself as I followed the other passengers to the baggage claim. Then it seemed like it took forever for luggage to start sliding down the chute and onto the carousel, which gave the anxious feeling the opportunity to swell and morph into something closer to full-fledged dread.

My suitcase finally tumbled onto the conveyor belt, though as soon as it did, I wished I could delay until I was in a mental state that was more likely to make a favorable impression on estranged relatives. But instead I pushed through the doors to the terminal, where Charity had told Thad she'd pick me up. (I'd refused to speak to her directly, since I'd still been trying to convince everyone I wasn't an orphan and had no intention of going to New York.)

Nobody rushed over to greet me, but I figured it would take a while to locate my aunt in the crowd, especially since I had no idea what she even looked like. All I had to go on was an old snapshot I'd found in a folder labeled PERSONAL MEMORABILIA filed between PALO ALTO CONSERVATION LEAGUE and PRIUS (TOYOTA) in my mother's home office.

The photo was of three girls on a sandy beach, and I'd recognized one of them as T.K. right away. She still wears her hair in the same shiny brown bob, and I've seen the same impatient expression on her face more times than I can count, usually while she's helping with my science homework. I'm okay at most subjects, but science is pretty much a lost cause.

Anyhow, my mother was probably younger than I am now when the picture was taken, and the two other girls looked even younger than that. The middle one had blond braids and a big fake beauty-pageant smile, while the smallest one was squinting her green eyes at the camera and scowling underneath a tangle of black curls. Neither of them looked anything like each other or like T.K., though there was something oddly familiar about the one with dark hair. But I didn't even know for sure they were her sisters, and if they were, who knew what they'd look like now?

Either way, I found myself scanning the crowd for anyone

with hair matching one of the two girls in the picture. There was a blondish woman, but she was too old to be my aunt, and she was with a man who was even older. As I watched, they started waving and smiling, and a younger blond woman lugging a matching blond toddler shouted a hello and hurried in their direction. A tired-looking guy who was probably her husband trailed behind with their bags.

The stream of travelers flowed around me and peeled off in groups of two and three and four. As the crowd grew smaller, the thick feeling that had been in my throat off and on for the last week came back, but I swallowed and kept looking.

When nobody was left but a man with a sign that said BIG APPLE LIMOS, I tried to convince myself that Thad must have misunderstood and that my aunt would be waiting for me outside. But outside I saw only a straggling taxi line and people making their way to the parking garage.

As a general rule, I believe that panic is a healthy response to being stranded in a strange city in the middle of the night, but it also seemed like freaking out wasn't an option just then. So I tried to stave off the panic by thinking what my mother would do.

T.K. approaches every problem with steady, cool logic. This comes a lot less easily for me, but now I did my best to channel her levelheaded calm. There was probably a perfectly reasonable explanation for my aunt not being there, and a simple phone call was all it would take to straighten everything out.

Even though T.K. considers it "an invasion of privacy and lapse in common courtesy" to call someone after ten P.M., I thought she'd okay it under the circumstances, so I dialed the number Charity had given Thad. And I broke another of T.K.'s rules of phone etiquette by not hanging up after five rings, which she says is long enough to give someone a chance to get to the phone or for voice mail to pick up but not long enough to be obnoxious.

It was eight whole rings before an automated voice came on to tell me that "the subscriber you have called is not available at this time." Then another automated voice came on and said, "The mailbox for this subscriber is full" before hanging up on me.

I stared at my phone. Then I checked the number and dialed again, but I got the same result.

At this point, no amount of swallowing could get rid of the thick feeling in my throat. It was also getting harder to keep channeling my mother, especially since Nora had spent so much time warning me about how careful I needed to be in a place like New York, where even the most harmless-looking person could be packing heat and intent on criminal mayhem.

But the next step was still pretty obvious. After all, I had Charity's address, and Thad had given me a bunch of twenties back at the airport in San Francisco. So I took my roller bag by the handle and went to join the taxi line with as much poise as I could scrape together.

I've traveled a lot for someone my age — my dad took me to India once, and we'd gone snowboarding a bunch of times in places like Colorado and Utah. One Christmas break we went to Hawaii, and we even convinced T.K. to come with us, though she refused to surf and spent the entire vacation sitting under a beach umbrella, slathered in sunscreen and working on her laptop.

But I'd never been to New York before. For the first fifteen minutes it looked like any other city, and we sped along a series of highways lined with residential neighborhoods and the occasional more industrial zone. Then the cab rounded a curve, and the Manhattan skyline popped up in the distance, just like in the movies, and I couldn't help but feel a little rush in spite of everything.

I managed to pick out the Empire State Building, its familiar outline lit in red, white, and blue, before we zoomed up a ramp and onto the 59th Street Bridge, which I would've recognized from the first *Spider-Man* even if there hadn't been an electronic map on the back of the driver's seat. A purple blip on the screen represented the taxi, chewing its way across the East River like a real-life version of the old Pac-Man game Erin had hacked to work on her Wii.

The bridge spilled us out onto an expressway with the river to one side and a blur of buildings to the other. I'd just caught a glimpse of the Brooklyn Bridge and the skyscrapers of lower

Manhattan, and even the Statue of Liberty, planted on its own island in the harbor, when, without warning, the driver cut across two lanes of traffic. We raced down an exit ramp and onto a street still busy with cars and people hours after everyone in Palo Alto would've been in bed.

Snatches of music coming from other cars mixed with the sounds of honking traffic and sirens, and now that the taxi was moving more slowly and wind wasn't rushing in through the window, I could feel the humidity in the air. We passed block after block of stores and restaurants, a lot of them with signs in Spanish or Hebrew or Chinese.

Even though most of what I knew of New York came filtered through Hollywood, I'd still thought I had a pretty good handle on what different neighborhoods were supposed to look like. The Upper East Side was elegant apartment buildings, and Midtown was glass-and-steel corporate headquarters, and SoHo was chic restaurants and boutiques. But we were now on the Lower East Side heading toward TriBeCa — at least, that's where the purple blip on the map was headed — and the confusion of people and languages reminded me more of Mumbai or New Delhi than anything I'd seen on TV.

Then the driver made a series of sharp turns, and suddenly the crowds and the noise were gone. "Fifteen Laight," he announced, jerking the taxi to a stop on a particularly deserted cobblestone street.

This was the first thing he'd said to me the entire ride — he'd spent most of it on his cell phone talking in what I was pretty sure was Urdu. But he helped get my bag out of the trunk, and when I paid him, he insisted on giving some of the money back, saying I'd tipped too much.

"I'll wait until you get inside," he offered, and I have to admit, I was glad he did. Now I understood why the taxi dispatcher at the airport had looked so surprised when I told her where I was going.

I'd never heard of Laight Street the way I'd heard of Park Avenue, but I knew from my mother that her parents were wealthy, so I'd assumed my aunts were, too, and that Charity's address would be just as fancy as Patience's.

But the building definitely didn't look fancy. If anything, it looked like a warehouse, and not the kind that had been made over into condos with a Starbucks and a dry cleaner in the lobby, like the ones I'd seen in San Francisco. There was no doorman like on *Gossip Girl* or even a neat, glass-enclosed directory like the apartment buildings I'd been to in Palo Alto. There was just a plastic intercom panel with a handful of names written on stickers and peeling pieces of tape.

The topmost label said **TRUESDALE — #5** in bold capital letters, and I took a deep breath as I reached out to press the button next to it. I wasn't sure what I'd do if nobody answered. Did hotels take unaccompanied minors?

But then I heard the speaker click on.

"Is this the Truesdale resi —" I started to ask, but before I could finish, the speaker clicked off and the door's lock buzzed open.

The cabdriver gave me a wave, put the taxi in gear, and disappeared around a corner.

Three

The heavy steel door led into a small foyer with an elevator to one side and a staircase to the other. The elevator was the kind that needed a key to set it in motion, but nobody came rushing down with a key, so after a minute I picked up my suitcase and headed for the stairs.

Between surfing and snowboarding and playing soccer at school, I like to think I'm in pretty good shape, but my pulse was beating hard when I finally reached the landing on the fifth floor. Though that might also have been because I was completely furious.

I probably should've been relieved to be safely inside, but as soon as the front door shut behind me, all the anxiety and dread erupted into pure, unadulterated rage. I'd been the ultimate in cool resourcefulness back at the airport. I hadn't panicked or done anything silly. There'd been no hysteria or accosting of random strangers, telling them my life story and throwing myself on their mercy. I'd gotten into a taxi and gotten myself here, with a minimum of fuss and as if I did that sort of thing all the time. T.K. would've been proud.

But instead of effusive apologies, or at the very least an explanation, I'd been greeted by an anonymous buzzer and the world's steepest stairs. And the single door on the fifth floor, the door with a big 5 scrawled on it in what looked like spray paint, remained closed.

I began counting backward from ten to get my temper under control, but as I counted I just got more and more angry. I knew that suddenly being responsible for the care of a sixteen-year-old girl might not have been what my aunt had planned — it sure wasn't what I'd planned, either — but it seemed like she could've said something instead of just flaking, and preferably before I flew across an entire continent.

There wasn't a doorbell, which was fine, because pounding on the door felt good even if it did make my knuckles hurt. Given how things were going, I half expected nobody to answer, so I wasn't that surprised when nobody did.

I was leaning against the door, trying to figure out what my mother would do next, when I spotted a sign taped to the banister of the next flight of stairs. **WE'RE ON THE ROOF**, it said, in the same handwriting as the label next to the buzzer downstairs. There was also an arrow, pointing up, as if whoever made the sign thought maybe I couldn't read.

I said a few of the sort of words that T.K. thinks are "indicative of a limited vocabulary and lack of imagination" before following the arrow up the final set of stairs. These let out onto another small landing and yet another heavy metal door.

I glared at the door, not even wanting to consider the possibility of nobody being on the other side. Then I pushed it open and stepped into the dazzling brightness of full day.

It took a second for my eyes to adjust, at which point I realized that the brightness was from banks of brilliant white lights. Extension cords snaked around my feet, and a bunch of glamorous-looking people in tuxes and ball gowns stood posed in little groups under the lights.

But nobody noticed me, because they were all focused on a skinny man in black. "NO NO NO!" he was yelling. "Zat is not vat I vant!" He had spiky blond hair and a long beaky nose, and he wore a scarf around his neck even though it must have been ninety degrees out. One end flowed behind him as he swept from group to group, and I had the feeling he'd spent a lot of time in front of a mirror figuring out how to make it flow that way.

"Zere!" he commanded, repositioning somebody an inch or two so he faced at a slight angle to the others. "And zere!" He made a minuscule adjustment to the tilt of a woman's head. Then he stepped back to admire his work, and I saw that a guy with a huge camera stood behind him, waiting to start filming.

"Zat is better," said the man in black. "Now, remember, it is a party, but you are sad. It is a celebration, but you are mourning. You are eager, but also vistful."

"Dieter!" a woman cried out from next to the cameraman. "Come on already. We're losing the light." Which made no sense to me. I mean, unless they were running out of electricity. But maybe this was movie-speak for something else.

The man in black — Dieter, I assumed — turned toward the woman. "Ze art cannot be rushed, Gertrude," he said haughtily.

Gertrude, who was wearing a female version of Dieter's outfit, complete with the scarf, made a sound that was a combination of a grunt and a snort. "But the budget can be busted. We're already paying everyone here time-and-a-half."

Dieter sighed, but he clapped his hands together. "Vight, vight. Places, everyvone. Places!"

Nobody moved, probably because they were already in the places he'd put them.

"Vight. Ready and — ACTION!"

Immediately, the crowd came to life. And almost as immediately, Dieter yelled, "CUT!"

"Now what?" demanded Gertrude.

"HER! Ze face! It is mesmerizing!" And before I knew what was happening, Dieter had my chin in his hand and was turning my head first one way and then the other.

"Mesmerizing" was pretty much the last word I'd ever used to describe myself — mostly I was just short — so I probably should've been flattered, but I was too busy being completely mortified. There must have been fifty beautifully dressed and made-up strangers on that roof, and they were all staring right at me. And none of them could possibly know that the only reason I was wearing the jeans and T-shirt I had on was that Nora had packed all of the clothes I actually liked, or that my nose wasn't usually such a striking shade of beet but I'd forgotten to use sunblock on my last trip to Ross's Cove.

It also wasn't like I could explain any of this with Dieter's fingers clamped around my jaw. "Ve must find her a part in ze scene," he declared.

"Fine," said Gertrude, but she didn't sound like she really thought so. In fact, she sounded like she was ready to throttle Dieter, and potentially me. "But she has to sign the release."

I tried to say something, but all I could manage was an ineffectual mumble. For such a scrawny guy, Dieter had an impressive grip.

"You are over eighteen, right?" Gertrude asked, stalking up and thrusting a clipboard in my face.

"No," I said, finally managing to free my chin from Dieter's grasp. "I'm sixteen."

Gertrude looked at me as if I'd been born when I had on purpose, just to make her life difficult. "Why is the agency sending us minors?" she said to Dieter. "We can't use her."

"But she's perfect. Ve MUST use her," Dieter insisted. "Vere is Zarley? ZARLEY!"

An especially glamorous dark-haired woman broke loose from one of the carefully arranged groups and made her way toward us, her red satin dress shimmering under the lights.

"What's the problem?" she asked brightly.

"This is the problem," growled Gertrude, pointing at me.

"I must have zis girl in ze film," said Dieter. "But she is ze minor, so she can't sign ze release."

"That's all right, one of her parents can sign ze — I mean, *the* — release." The woman turned to me. "We'll just need you to get a signature from your mom or dad."

"I can't," I said.

"She says she can't," the woman reported to Dieter and Gertrude.

"Then she can't be in the film," Gertrude said to Dieter, in a "so there" sort of way.

"But she MUST be in ze film!" Dieter said stubbornly.

Gertrude heaved a sigh of exasperation. "This is what we get for working with amateurs."

The woman in the red dress didn't seem to appreciate either of us being called amateurs. She put her hands on her hips and her voice took on a steely edge. "Excuse me?"

Maybe it was her tone, or her height — she was nearly a foot taller than me — or maybe it was simply the way her green eyes flashed as she spoke, but she was suddenly imposing. Gertrude swallowed whatever she was planning to say, and Dieter moved closer to her, like she might come in handy as a human shield.

Satisfied, the woman turned her attention back to me. "Sorry it won't work out this time," she said. "But maybe you can be in the next film."

The steeliness was gone from her tone, and her smile was kind, but it was also dismissive, and somehow the dismissiveness was the last straw. It had been a long day, complete with more mood swings than I usually have in any given week, and I'd been teetering on the brink since the plane landed. I put my own hands on my own hips and let all of the words I'd been holding back pour out.

"I don't want to be in this film or the next film or any film! I don't want to be here at all! It wasn't my idea to leave California, and my home, and my friends, and my school, and my entire LIFE, and to fly three thousand miles to live with someone I've never met who doesn't even pick me up at the airport when she says she's going to. And I can't get permission from my parents because my dad is dead, and everyone thinks my mother is, too —"

That's when I ran out of words, which was just as well, because Dieter cracked up. Which isn't exactly the reaction you want when you're trying to show you're a force to be reckoned with.

"I can see how hilarious this must be for you," I said to him.

He tried, unsuccessfully, to stop laughing. "It's just zat you are like ze Mini-Me. You know, from ze *Austin Powers*. Not an artistic vork, but very entertaining is zis film —"

Meanwhile, the woman in the red dress was staring at me. "Who *are* you?" she asked.

"I'm Delia," I said. "Who are *you*?"

"Don't be silly," she said. "You can't be Delia. Delia's coming tomorrow."

"It *is* tomorrow," I said.

"But Delia's flight doesn't get in until five past twelve. That's hours away."

"My flight did get in at five past twelve," I said. "Twelve midnight."

"Midnight?" she said in disbelief. "What kind of flight gets in at midnight? Flights get in at noon, not midnight."

I didn't point out that a plane would've had to leave the West Coast at three in the morning to arrive in New York at noon. I only said, "My flight got in at midnight."

"Then you're Delia?" she asked. "But when did — how did — I mean — you're absolutely sure you're Delia?"

She ran a hand through her hair, and a black curl came loose from its knot. And all at once, I saw her resemblance to the scowling little girl in the picture and realized why the little girl had seemed familiar.

She looked a lot like me.

The thick feeling was suddenly back in my throat, making it hard to say anything, so I just nodded.

Her mouth formed a perfect red *O* as realization washed over her. Then, slowly, her hands fell from her hips and the *O* melted into a wide, warm smile.

"Well, Delia," she said. "I'm your aunt Charley."

And when she hugged me, it felt like hitting a wave just right.

Four

For a few seconds the next morning I forgot where I was. All of my dreams had been set in Palo Alto, and I could smell bacon, which happens a lot in the morning at home. While T.K. doesn't have any of the standard vices like smoking or gambling, she does have a serious bacon habit. So with my eyes shut and the bacon-scented air, it was easy to imagine I was in my own bed. But once I opened my eyes it was immediately clear I was somewhere else entirely.

My room at home mostly reflects my mother's taste, which means the palette is white on white, with the occasional splash of white to keep things interesting. I'd raised the possibility of alternative color schemes on several occasions, but T.K. believes that "a monochromatic environment promotes focus and intellectual rigor."

If that was true, then I might as well say farewell to focus and intellectual rigor while I was at Charley's. Here the paint on the walls was a glimmering silver, and brightly colored silks hung at the windows. The rich blues and greens of the curtains should have clashed with the pinks and purples on the bed, but somehow it worked.

Charley had told me the previous night that she had the curtains and bedspread made from material she found in a store in Jackson Heights, a neighborhood where a lot of South Asians live. She'd redone the room just for me, which was incredibly nice on such short notice, but I had the feeling she'd thought I'd be more exotic, or at least a bit more in touch with my father's Indian roots. I guess she had no way of knowing that every other person in Silicon Valley is of Indian descent or related to an Internet tycoon, and that frequently they're both. I'm actually considered pretty mainstream.

Between the hour and the fact that she was supposed to be coproducing, starring in, and serving as the casting director, location manager, and production designer for the movie being shot on the roof, we hadn't had much time to talk the night before. Charley had told me about Jackson Heights and also a bunch of stuff about Dieter's brilliant creative vision before promising we'd catch up in the morning and rushing back upstairs.

I'd thought I'd be too wired to sleep, but as soon as I'd seen the cozy-looking bed, a wave of exhaustion broke over me. It took all of the energy I had left to drag a toothbrush across my teeth and change into pajamas. The only reason I'd bothered with the toothbrush was that T.K. has done such a good job scaring me about gum disease.

Now the clock on the bedside table said it was after ten, and the bacon smell reminded me that it had been a long time since

I'd last eaten. My pajamas consisted of a tank top and sweat-pants, but Charley seemed like the informal type — she wouldn't even let anyone call her Charity ("I mean, do I look like a Victorian spinster?" she'd said when I asked) — so I decided it would be okay not to get more dressed and went in search of food.

The loft took up the whole fifth floor of the building, and most of it was a huge open space. My room was down a short hallway, and Charley's room was down another, but just about everything else was in the main room, including a kitchen area at one end, a big round table in the middle, and a mismatched collection of sofas and chairs at the other end. A long row of oversized windows framed a view of the buildings across the street.

The kitchen counter was piled with grocery bags, and Charley was at the stove, trying to turn bacon with tongs that still had a price tag dangling from them.

"Delia, hi," she said, looking up with a cheery smile. "I hope you're hungry." She gestured casually with the tongs, as if try-ing to imply that she cooked all the time, but just then a drop of sizzling fat flew up from the pan and nailed the inside of her wrist, and she let loose with a few words that neatly proved how wrong T.K. was about swearing and a lack of imagination.

"Can I help?" I asked.

"Everything's under control," she assured me, apparently

unaware that the pan was starting to smoke. She chattered on as I tried to remember if I knew anything about putting out grease fires.

I shouldn't have worried about the pan, but it would be a while before I realized that just about everything Charley did turned out all right, no matter how inevitably disaster seemed to loom. I learned much more quickly that she liked to talk. A lot.

"There's fresh orange juice — do you like orange juice?" she asked. "Some people like grapefruit juice better, and I know it's supposed to be really good for you, but it makes my mouth feel all puckered. I also picked up bagels and cream cheese. I wanted your first meal here to be authentically New York, so it was either bagels or ordering in from the taco place, and since the taco place doesn't open for another hour, bagels won. And everyone likes bagels. Except for people on a low-carb diet. But even they like bagels, they just don't eat them. You're not on a low-carb diet, are you?"

I wasn't sure which question to answer first, but it didn't matter, because Charley was already on to the next series of topics, which included: her love of carbs, how her love of carbs almost made training for a marathon seem appealing except for what it would do to her toenails, how important toenails were for open-toed shoes, not to mention peep-toes and sandals, and how sore her feet were from standing around the previous night while Dieter shot the same scene over and over again.

By now, we were at the table with enough food for a small team of sumo wrestlers and Charley took a big bite of bagel, which gave me my first opportunity to say much of anything. And what I most wanted to know was how she and my C-Span-watching, loafer-wearing mother could possibly be sisters, but asking which one was adopted didn't seem like the most polite way to start a conversation. So since all of the other adults I knew liked talking about their work, I asked about her movie career instead.

She laughed. "Don't let Dieter or Gertrude hear you call it a 'movie,' whatever you do. It's an independent *film*, darling," she said in a mock-affected way. "And I wouldn't call it a career, either. It's just something I'm doing right now."

"Oh," I said, lacking context for this. In Silicon Valley, people tend to define themselves by their profession. It's not about money, either — T.K. has a trust fund from her great-great-grandparents or something like that, and she's made plenty on her own, but it still hasn't stopped her from being a total worka-holic. "Then what do you usually do?" I asked Charley.

"Usually?" she repeated, as if the word was foreign to her. "I don't know if I've ever had a 'usually.' That sounds sort of . . . bleak."

"Well, what did you do first?"

"You mean after Brown?"

"You went to Brown? But don't Truesdales get disowned if they don't go to Princeton?"

"No, your mother was kind enough to break that mold. At least as far as college. You should have seen the fit your grandparents threw when I told them about the Peace Corps. Then I almost did get cut off."

"No way," I said, impressed. "You were in the Peace Corps?"

"Sure," she said, as if everyone joined the Peace Corps, and as if the Betsey Johnson dress she was wearing was standard issue for Peace Corps alums. "I spent a few years in Ghana, teaching HIV and AIDS prevention. Then I traveled around Africa for a while. The different cultures and climates were fascinating, and I liked the animals so much that I decided to go back to school to be a zoologist. But it turns out they make you study every single kind. Giraffes and elephants are one thing, but who can get excited about mollusks, except maybe the French? And they'll eat anything."

"So then came the movies? I mean, films?"

"Oh, no. There was a lot of stuff in between. Let's see," she said, using her fingers to tick off occupations. "Africa, and then grad school. Then I got interested in Eastern medicine, but it turns out that I'm a bit squeamish about needles so acupuncture class was a problem. What else? There was the magazine. And the gallery, of course. But the only people buying art back then were Wall Street types. I can't even begin to describe what stiffs those hedge-fund goons were. Their idea of a good time was *golf.*" She shuddered. "It's like the crash was some sort of divine punishment for bad taste."

"And then what?" I asked. She still had a few fingers left.

"And then the film, I guess. Unless I kill Gertrude first. Don't you think Gertrude looks more like a Helga than a Gertrude?"

As if on cue, a cell phone began ringing from somewhere under the bags on the counter. "Speak of the devil," said Charley. "That's probably her, even though we're supposed to be taking the day off."

She found the phone and checked the caller ID. "Ack!"

"Helga?" I asked.

"Even worse. I think I'll let voice mail pick this up."

"What's worse than Helga?"

"The Wicked Witch of the Upper East Side. Though maybe you should forget I said that. I don't want to scare you before you've even met her. But it does seem only fair to warn you. The Flying Monkeys are pretty special, too."

"Who's the Wicked Witch of the Upper East Side? And who're the Flying Monkeys?"

"Your other aunt and her kids," said Charley. "Patty's twins, Gwyneth and Grey. That's Grey with an *E* — they went for the British spelling, just in case the name itself wasn't pretentious enough. But don't worry. We're safe for now. I never give out my home number, and especially not to family."

The words were no sooner out of her mouth than the land-line phone on a side table started to ring. Charley jumped, startled, then she snatched up the receiver and checked the screen. "How?" she cried. "How does she do it? Nobody has this number. It's unlisted. I'm not even sure *I* know what it is."

There was a click as the answering machine picked up the call, and a moment later a voice began streaming from the speaker. It could've just been distortion from the machine, but the woman who spoke sounded like she was sucking on something sour:

> *Charity, are you there? Are you there? Are you screening your calls again? Are you? You know, it's really very rude to screen your own sister like this —*

"What does she expect when this is the sort of thing she calls to say?" asked Charley, sinking back into her chair.

> *— and the voice mail on your mobile phone is full, which is very irresponsible. What if somebody needed to reach you urgently? I don't know what Temperance was thinking. As we all know, you can't even manage to raise a Chia Pet —*

"She'll never let me forget that, will she?" said Charley.

> *— much less a child. And there are several important things we need to discuss about Cordelia. First, I've called Prescott, and they're expecting you both in the headmaster's office first thing Tuesday morning. Tuesday as in tomorrow. Now,*

Jeremy and I had to pull a lot of strings to get a place for Cordelia at such late notice —

"Jeremy's her husband," Charley explained. "They're perfect for each other. Which should tell you a lot."

— fortunately, the Paulson girl had to enter a long-term treatment facility for her eating disorder, so a space opened up in the junior class. Now, I expect you to be punctual, and I expect you to wear something appropriate. And you know what I mean by appropriate. I haven't bought Cordelia's uniform yet since I didn't know her size, but she can wear one of Gwyneth's old ones in the meantime. Though we may have to let it out. Gwyneth's so willowy — she takes after me that way. Second, we'll expect you at the beach house in Southampton —

"No!" said Charley, a look of terror on her face.

— this weekend. That includes you as well as Cordelia, and given the circumstances, I don't think anybody will have any patience for one of your excuses. I suggest you be there, and I suggest you be on time. You know, there's a reason why we keep giving you watches for Christmas. You might want to start wearing them. The gold Patek Philippe from last year is a beautiful piece. And it was certainly

a more appropriate gift than the rug-hooking kit you
gave me —

At this point, Charley had her head in her hands and was moaning softly.

— Third, I've made an appointment for Cordelia with Dr. Chiswick. I hardly think you're qualified to provide the sort of support that a girl needs during such a traumatic time, and he's considered to be the finest child psych —

Charley leaped up and hit the OFF button on the answering machine. "And that," she said, "is your aunt Patience."

I didn't think it was a coincidence that she'd stopped the message playing when she did. "Look," I said, "there's no need to send me to a shrink." I pushed my chair back and began clearing the table.

"Why don't we figure that out later?" Charley said after a moment. "Once you've settled in a bit."

"Really. It's a waste of time," I said.

"Delia," Charley began awkwardly, "I hate to agree with Patty about anything, but it might not be such a bad idea. The death of a par — well, it's a hard thing to deal with."

"But I don't have anything to deal with."

"What do you mean?"

"This is only temporary. T.K. will be back."

Charley was silent, clearly trying to figure out what to say to that. I should've been surprised to see her at a loss for words, but I was too focused on making my point. "You must think I'm crazy or in denial or something," I said, after I'd explained about the label maker and the lack of proof and everything. "Everyone at home does, too. But it's all a mistake."

"I don't think you're crazy," said Charley, even though her tone suggested she wasn't sure but was trying not to show it. "But are you sure you don't want to talk to someone more . . . skilled in this area? It might help."

"What I really want is to find my mother, and I don't see how a doctor's going to do that."

She hesitated, but then she nodded. "Okay. If that's what you want. But you should let me know if you change your mind."

"I won't," I said.

She came to join me in the kitchen, loading the plates I rinsed into the dishwasher. "Now, more importantly, what are you going to wear for your first day tomorrow?"

I'd already freaked her out enough, so I didn't point out that it didn't matter since I'd be back at West Palo Alto High as soon as T.K. returned. I just said, "I don't have a lot to choose from until my boxes get here. Besides — it sounds like I have to wear a uniform."

"You can't really think I'd let you go to Prescott?" said Charley, like Prescott was some sort of cult or polygamist compound. "I barely survived the place myself. No, Patty's not the

37

only one who can pull strings. I asked around, and I heard about the most fabulous new school, with a revolutionary alternative curriculum. That's where you'll be going, Delia."

"What's alternative about it?" I asked. "Or revolutionary?"

"Everything. Conventional education can be so structured and limiting, but the Center for Academic and Spiritual Growth believes in nurturing a sense of self-direction in its students. I've heard Brad and Angelina are thinking about sending Maddox there when he's old enough. But we'd better get going. We have an outfit to plan. Some of my things might work, though they might be a little long. Or wait — I have a better idea! Have you ever been to Scoop? Or Barney's Co-Op?"

"T.K. hates shopping," I admitted. "Mostly we just order my clothes from catalogs."

Charley had been pretty calm during the entire T.K. discussion, but now she almost dropped the plate she was holding. "Catalogs?"

"Catalogs," I confirmed. "She likes them because they present a finite range of options."

"That is an absolute tragedy," she said. "But one I'm uniquely qualified to remedy. I can be ready to go in four minutes. What about you?"

Five

Palo Alto isn't exactly a fashion-forward sort of town, but I'd always considered myself on the more stylish end of the spectrum. I mean, it was true that most of my clothes came from catalogs, but at least they came from different catalogs than the ones my mother uses to order her khakis and sweater sets.

It turns out that the stylish end of the Palo Alto spectrum stops where the frumpy end of the New York spectrum begins. And while Charley might have been a little scattered about things like when her temporarily orphaned niece's flight would be arriving from the West Coast, there was nothing scattered about her in a retail environment. She attacked each store like an invading army, plucking items from racks with military precision and marshaling salespeople like a drill sergeant.

We shopped our way from TriBeCa to SoHo and from there to the Meatpacking District, with a stop in the middle at a restaurant called Balthazar for *pommes frites* and profiteroles because Charley said we needed to keep our strength up. Most of the places we went were completely unfamiliar to me — stores like Olive & Bette's and Intermix — and the day flew by in a blur of dressing rooms and three-way mirrors. By the time we got back to the loft, I had a whole new wardrobe, and it had been me vetoing the things I thought were too edgy. At home, T.K. does all the vetoing.

We picked up tacos for dinner and stayed up way too late figuring out what I should wear the next day. This was mostly because of Charley. I like clothes as much as the next person — in fact, I probably like them a lot more — but worrying about the impression I was going to make at a new school was pretty low on my list of priorities.

Charley, on the other hand, was like a little girl with her first Barbie. She insisted that I try on every possible combination of the items we'd purchased, and it wasn't just because she was trying to keep my mind off my mother, either. She was seriously intense when it came to planning outfits.

We eventually settled on a Paul and Joe shirt in a reddish-pink color ("too fabulous with your skin tone," said Charley) and a pair of Rag & Bone skinny jeans, but deciding on my top and bottom took so long that we ended up going to bed without resolving footwear. Which meant that we had to reconvene in my room directly after breakfast the next morning to figure out which pair of new shoes worked best with the clothes we'd picked out.

So that's where we were when a car screeched to a halt on the street below, triggering a bunch of nearby car alarms. We could hear the noise five floors up, but neither of us paid much attention — we were too caught up in debating a pair of Christian Louboutin ankle boots I'd vetoed but Charley had bought anyhow.

"I just don't know if they're me," I was saying. I'd embraced most of Charley's choices, but it was an extra-long leap from J. Crew flip-flops to Louboutins, and I wasn't sure I was ready for it.

"They can be you," said Charley enthusiastically.

"Maybe you should try them instead?" I suggested.

"I wear a size ten," she pointed out. "You wear a seven. And, lucky you, these just happen to be a size seven."

"Won't I be late if we don't leave soon?" I asked, thinking maybe I could distract her.

"The Center doesn't believe in strict timetables or taking attendance or anything like that. It's impossible to be late."

I was still trying to get my head around a school where you couldn't be late when suddenly the determined clatter of high heels sounded in the living room.

"What's that?" I asked, on instant alert. It seemed like the wrong hour of day for a burglar, but Nora's warnings were still fresh in my mind — it was hard not to feel at least a small jolt of alarm.

"It couldn't be," said Charley in disbelief. The Louboutins slipped from her grasp.

The bedroom door crashed open against the wall, and I let out an involuntary shriek. A blond-haired woman in an austere black suit stood in the doorway. She was as thin and angular as a store mannequin, and diamond earrings the size of small boulders competed for attention with the massive diamond on her ring finger. A Louis Vuitton garment bag was slung over her arm.

Her glare landed on Charley. "What kind of absurd excuse for an academic institution is this supposed to be?" she said, brandishing a brochure for the Center for Academic and Spiritual Growth.

"How did you get in?" demanded Charley.

"With a key," said the woman. "Obviously."

"But who gave you a key?"

The woman didn't answer but just turned her icy blue eyes to me. "Cordelia?"

I was tempted to hide behind Charley, but I managed to restrain myself. "Um, yes?" I said.

"I'm Patience Truesdale-Babbitt. Your aunt. The one who's not utterly insane."

"It's nice to meet you," I said, though mostly it was terrifying.

"I'm also the aunt whose attorney just assured her that your mother's will definitely gives me final say over your education."

"But —" began Charley.

Patience spoke over Charley like she wasn't even there. "Me, and not my crackpot sister. So you can imagine my surprise when the registrar at Prescott informed me that said crackpot sister had made other arrangements — not to mention the inconvenience I've already endured this morning undoing those other arrangements. If you can call this" — she looked with distaste at the brochure — "this *place* an arrangement."

"But —" began Charley again.

Patience ignored her again. "Now, we're already behind schedule, and if you think that what you're wearing is appropriate, Cordelia, then you have been recklessly misled. Please hurry and put this on." And with that she unzipped the garment bag and yanked out a neatly pressed school uniform.

Charley gasped in horror, like there was a rattlesnake or cobra dangling from the hanger. Gingerly, she reached out a finger to touch the navy blazer. "It hasn't changed a bit," she said. "And it's still that same awful material. I tried to burn mine after I graduated but it only melted. You'd think for such a fancy place they'd insist on natural fibers."

"Prescott is the finest private day school in Manhattan, and it is an honor to wear its colors," said Patience sternly, thrusting the uniform in my direction. "Cordelia, I'll wait for you in the other room while you change. And please don't dawdle — the clock is ticking."

The door slammed shut behind her, and Charley immediately reached for the phone to get her own lawyer involved. But I stopped her before she could start dialing.

I didn't want to hurt her feelings, but I thought I might as well go somewhere halfway decent while I was in New York so that I wouldn't be completely behind when I got back to my old school. And I had to admit, I'd had doubts about the Center for Academic and Spiritual Growth, too. After all, the brochure began with "Greetings, Voyagers!" and that was pretty out there, even for a Californian. I was starting to see why my mother had put certain decisions in Patience's hands — she was definitely scary — but she might be useful to have around in situations like this.

It took some convincing, though I think that was mostly because Charley objected automatically to anything Patience wanted. She only yielded after I promised I'd let her know immediately if I had second thoughts about Prescott. She also insisted on drawing me a map of her favorite escape routes from when she was a student. "You never know when this might come in handy," she said, zipping it into a pocket of my book bag.

"Maybe I should have some garlic and a wooden stake, too," I said. "Or do you have one of those revolvers that shoot silver bullets?"

"You won't be thinking that's so funny when you see what you've signed yourself up for," she warned, just as we heard a long scraping noise from the other room, followed by the squeal of something heavy and metal being dragged across the floor.

"I don't believe it," said Charley in amazement. "Is she really rearranging the furniture?"

As if to answer her question there was another scraping noise, and then a thud and the sound of shattering glass.

"Patty, you better not be doing what I think you're doing," Charley yelled in a tone that made her sound as scary as Patience. She was already halfway through the door.

I had the feeling that it might be dangerous to leave my aunts alone together, so I hurried to change into the navy-and-red plaid kilt and the blazer with its gold Prescott Day School crest. After the jeans and top we'd chosen so carefully, it all felt itchy and strange and weirdly formal. Even the Louboutins seemed a lot more appealing now that I'd seen the lace-up saddle shoes that went with the uniform.

There was more scraping and another thud from the other room, and also the clipped tones people use to argue when they're trying to argue and still keep their voices down. I knew I should probably get out there before things got any worse, but I paused in front of the mirror.

My reflection looked like it belonged to a totally different girl than the one who'd been surfing Ross's Cove just a few short days ago. For a moment, I wondered what my dad would think, and what T.K. would think, too, if either of them could see me now.

Then I went to join my aunts.

Six

It was probably a good thing I got there when I did. Charley and Patience were eyeing each other like feral cats stalking the same prey, and I was pretty sure my presence was the only thing standing between them and physical violence.

Patience seemed a bit miffed that not only did I fit into her daughter's castoffs, everything was a little loose, but she wasted no time shuttling me out of the loft and into the elevator. Charley was calling after me even as the elevator doors closed, reminding me to phone if I needed anything, or wanted her to come get me, or craved anything special for dinner, or just wanted to talk.

Downstairs, a driver was waiting to whisk us away in a big German car. Patience ("Do not — *not* — call me Patty," she informed me briskly as the car pulled away from the curb) spent the entire ride uptown extolling the virtues of Prescott, pausing only long enough to occasionally mutter under her breath about her crackpot sister and Chia Pets. On the bright side, at least I didn't have to work too hard to keep up my end of the conversation.

Prescott occupied two adjoining stone-and-brick town houses on a leafy side street in the East 80s, not far from Central Park. Patience insisted on accompanying me to the headmaster's office, and she strode through the front door like she owned the place. I got the sense that she thought I'd try to make a break for it if her attention lapsed for even a second. I was quickly learning that my aunt took her responsibilities very, very seriously, and it was more than a little unnerving to find out that I was one of them.

Prescott had marble floors and dark wood paneling where my school at home had Mexican tile and Mission-style stucco, but otherwise it felt the same, with metal lockers lining the hallway and bulletin boards and posters on the walls. Even the headmaster, a staid-looking older man named Mr. Seton, reminded me of Mr. Olivaro, the principal at West Palo Alto, though Mr. Seton wore a suit and tie where Mr. Olivaro always wore khakis and a button-down shirt.

Mr. Seton only convinced Patience to leave after assuring her that he'd personally supervise my registration, and he seemed nearly as relieved as I was when she finally took off, though he probably had a better poker face. On the way to the registrar's office, he told me he'd been at Prescott for more than thirty years, which meant he'd known my mother and her sisters when they were students. "All so different, and with such unique personalities," he said, though the way he said "unique" made it sound like a euphemism for something less diplomatic.

47

T.K. had graduated while Patience was still in the Middle School and Charley in the Lower School, but they'd all left their marks. I saw T.K.'s name on a plaque listing the class valedictorian for each year on one wall, and on another wall there was a photograph of a teenage Patience posing with a trophy she'd won in a debate tournament. Mr. Seton even showed me a side door that he said was Charley's favorite escape route for cutting class. I knew from Charley herself that her favorite was actually a window on the opposite end of the building, but it didn't seem wise to correct him.

He deposited me with the registrar, and if the uniform hadn't already clued me in, the schedule she handed me made it clear that Prescott was going to be a lot more challenging than the Center for Academic and Spiritual Growth was likely to have been. My classes were nearly identical to what they'd be at home, with only one exception: Instead of computer science, at Prescott I'd been enrolled in drama.

"I'm sorry, dear," the registrar said when I asked, but she sounded more surprised than sorry. "That's the only elective that would fit with the rest of your schedule. Most of the students love drama, you know. Mr. Dudley, the instructor, is a favorite around here."

I had to admit to being a tiny bit curious about drama. But I could also hear T.K.'s voice in my ear, telling me that Mr. Dudley might be a favorite, but drama didn't help much on the SATs. At least it wouldn't start until the following week, since he was wrapping up a one-man show in summer stock, whatever that was. By then, maybe everything would be back to normal or, at the very least, I'd have figured out a way to change my schedule.

"Do you want directions to the science lab?" the registrar asked. "Your advanced physics class has already started, but I'm sure Dr. Penske will excuse your tardiness this one time — oh —" she said as my phone rang in my bag. "We don't allow our students to use their cell phones in the building. You'll have to turn that off, dear."

I quickly silenced the ringing and listened politely while she told me how I could find the lab. But as soon as I was in the hallway, and since I was already late anyhow, I ducked into the nearest stairwell to see who'd phoned.

I'd texted the previous day with both Justin and Erin, but it was still pretty early in the morning on the West Coast for one of them to be trying me, and I had a funny feeling about this call that I couldn't quite explain.

The log on the caller ID just said "Out of Area" so I knew it couldn't be anyone whose number was already programmed into my phone. There was a single voice mail waiting, and my fingers felt strangely stiff as I punched in my password. I tried to tell myself it would only be Thad, calling to nag about my executive training or something like that, but somehow I knew that wasn't it.

And it wasn't. At least, if it was, there was no way to tell.

Because all I could hear was static. I played the message over again, and then I played it a third time. But each time I heard the same thing: sixteen seconds of static.

I'd been so proud of how I hadn't cried once since that moment when Nora sat me down at our kitchen table, but now I felt a prickling in my eyes. I stared at the wall, willing the prickling to stop. Had I really thought it would be a message from my mother? The sudden shiver of doubt that swept through me was even worse than the threat of tears.

"Didn't anyone tell you that cell phones during school hours are strictly *verboten*?" asked a teasing male voice.

I started and spun around, but I didn't see anyone.

"Up here," he said.

A single figure was on the landing above. He was tall, with thick, sand-colored hair, and he leaned against the windowsill with casual ease. The sun poured through the glass behind him, gilding his outline, but even when he'd stepped out of the pool of light he still looked like a god.

Seven

My brain seemed to stop working, which meant I couldn't come up with a witty reply, or even a reply that would prove I was capable of doing anything other than standing frozen in place with my mouth gaping open. But I did manage to memorize the details, especially his eyes, which were the same gray-green as the Pacific on a cloudy morning.

Then he was gone, disappearing up and around the turn of the stairs. I could hear his footsteps above and the stairwell door swinging shut behind him.

I don't know how long I stood there before my brain started working again, but it was definitely longer than I'd care to admit. And once I'd recovered, I almost wished I hadn't, because that's when the embarrassment kicked in.

The good news, I guessed, was that I'd forgotten about crying, and also about that chilling shiver of doubt. And it's not like my tongue had been hanging out of my open mouth or I'd drooled or anything. But that didn't mean I wasn't mortified by my utter lack of cool.

I didn't have tons of experience on the romantic front — in fact, it would be a stretch to say I had *any* experience — but that had mostly been by choice. After all, I'd known nearly all of the guys at home since Palo Alto Montessori, so even the ones who weren't completely obsessed with hacking into top secret computer networks or becoming the next Mark Zuckerberg were hard to cast as romantic leads. Still, I'd always considered myself to be at least semicompetent socially.

But I'd just found out how pathetically wrong I was about that.

I was still a bit dazed as I returned the phone to my bag and went to find the science lab. I followed the registrar's directions up one corridor and down another, and I eventually reached the right door.

The teacher must have been expecting me, because as soon as he caught a glimpse of my face through the door's glass window he waved me in with an eagerness that was sort of alarming. He had thinning brown hair and there was chalk dust on his tie and sports coat.

"You must be Cordelia!" he boomed.

"Actually, it's Delia," I said. "Just Delia."

"Well, Just Delia — ha ha ha — I'm Dr. Penske. And I must say, this is a real honor. Class, do you know who our new student is?" He didn't wait for anyone to answer. "Delia is the daughter of T.K. Truesdale, who was not only a Prescott alumna but the genius behind TrueTech. I'm sure you've all heard of TrueTech."

Rows of blue-blazer-wearing students looked back at him, mostly with indifference. He was undaunted by the lack of response, nor did it seem to occur to him that T.K. might be a sensitive topic just now.

"If Delia has even half of her mother's talent, she'll be the star of our class," Dr. Penske blundered on. "Now, let's see. Who still needs a lab partner?"

"I do," volunteered a red-haired girl sitting at a table right up front.

"Perfect," said Dr. Penske. "Delia, Natalie's one of our best students, but I'm sure she'll have plenty to learn from you."

I doubted that I'd be able to teach her much of anything, especially not without T.K. around to tutor me, and I wasn't thrilled about the front-and-center placement, but I did my best to match Natalie's eager smile and slid into the empty seat beside her.

Dr. Penske resumed his lecture, and I even took out a note-book and pen. But I had a hard time concentrating in science under the most ideal circumstances — there was no way I could possibly focus at a time like this.

I mean, it wasn't like my mind hadn't already been crowded. Between worrying about T.K. and processing the move and everything that came with it, I'd had plenty to occupy my thoughts.

And now, just in case things hadn't been bad enough, the

Stairwell God had taken up residence, too. My head would probably explode if I added anything else to the mix.

So what was left of the class period slipped away with me mostly staring into space — even doodling was beyond me at that point. Meanwhile, Natalie took page after page of notes. As far as I could tell, she was writing down what Dr. Penske said verbatim, including the articles and prepositions, and pressing down with such force that the words were practically carved into the paper.

By the time the bell rang, she'd already used up one pen and was well on her way through the ink in a second. My notebook, on the other hand, was as pristine as if it was still on the shelf at Staples.

"What do you have next, Delia?" asked Natalie as we packed up our things. "Lunch?"

"I think so," I said, checking my schedule.

"Me, too. We can go together if you want."

"Sure," I said. "That would be great." No matter how little a person cares about making new friends — and I fully intended to be back lunching with Erin and Justin in the not-so-distant future — nobody wants to brave a foreign cafeteria alone.

At West Palo Alto High, the cafeteria was in its own wing of the school, and when the weather was good, which was almost always, we'd take our trays out to the picnic tables in the adjacent courtyard. In Manhattan, space was scarce, which meant that the Prescott cafeteria was crammed into the school's basement. Windows set high in the walls offered the occasional glimpse of feet walking by on the sidewalk above.

Natalie and I collected our food — there was sushi and lamb ragout and beet risotto but we both got grilled cheese — and found places at one of the long wooden tables. Based on the way she'd been sitting alone in class and Dr. Penske raving about what a good student she was, I'd assumed Natalie was the shy, bookish type.

But it turned out that Natalie was about as shy and bookish as an untrained puppy. And it also turned out that her interest in me was more than basic kindness or the need for a lab partner — she was fascinated by T.K. and pretty much anything else that had to do with Silicon Valley, and she questioned me with the same fierce intensity she'd used to take notes in class.

"Is it true your mom started TrueTech out of her dorm room in college?" she asked. "I'm dying to go to Stanford. MIT's my backup. What do people think of MIT on the West Coast? I heard the venture capitalists like Stanford grads better. The Google guys went to Stanford, didn't they? Do you know them? Have you been on their plane?"

On the drive uptown and without a hint of sarcasm, Patience had informed me that Prescott was the "preparatory institution of choice for the offspring of New York's power and social elite." So I'd expected kids at Prescott to be more into things like politics and fashion — or at least sneaking into clubs.

But sitting with Natalie was exactly like hanging out at home, though Erin and Justin already knew how many other things I'd rather talk about than the Google guys and their plane. Natalie even started telling me her start-up ideas and asking about how to attract investors.

"Are there a lot of people here who are interested in that sort of thing?" I asked.

"What sort of thing?"

"Start-ups and technology and stuff like that."

"I wish," she said mournfully. "Most of the kids here couldn't care less about accomplishing something. In fact, most of the kids here couldn't care less about anything. There's the drama crowd, and the jocks, and the stoners, like at any other school, but the popular kids or the in crowd, or whatever you want to call them, don't think it's cool to be into anything, except maybe acting bored and spending their parents' money." She lowered her voice. "I have my own name for them."

"What's that?" I asked.

She glanced around to make sure nobody else was listening. "I call them the Apathy Alliance." Then she did a double take, startled by something she glimpsed over my shoulder. "Speaking of which, guess who's heading this way. I wonder what they want." Disdain mixed with apprehension in her tone.

I twisted around in my seat and saw a tall, slender girl strolling toward us with a matching tall, slender guy. They

56

both had nearly white-blond hair, and there was something familiar about the cool blue gazes that looked me up and down.

"Cordelia?" said the girl. Her voice sounded hoarse, like it was rusty from lack of use.

"Delia," I said with a bright California smile. "I go by Delia."

"I'm Gwyneth. Your cousin. This is Grey. With an *E*. He's also your cousin. We're both seniors here." She spoke in a languorous monotone, completely stripped of inflection, and she managed to get the words out with the barest minimum of facial movement. Grey didn't speak at all.

I kept the smile going, trying to make up for their lack of enthusiasm with my own. "Hi. It's nice to meet you."

"Our mother wanted us to introduce ourselves and make sure you feel welcome," said Gwyneth as Grey stifled a yawn.

I said I did, but mostly I was busy trying to remember which movie had the villain whose superpower was putting people to sleep.

"Good. Then I suppose we'll see you this weekend in Southampton. Come on, Grey."

"Are they really your cousins?" asked Natalie as Gwyneth and Grey strolled out of the lunchroom.

"I guess so," I said. Inwardly, I was busy wondering how the same gene pool had produced T.K., Charley, Patience, the ennui twins, and me. There must have been some major mutations along the way.

"Well," she said, "Gwyneth is a charter member of the Apathy Alliance. So is Grey."

"Then who's the president? Or whatever an alliance has?" I asked.

"He's more than the president," said Natalie. "He's like the founder and the king and the Grand Pooh-Bah all rolled into one. If the Apathy Alliance were a galaxy, he'd be its sun. Your cousins would be orbiting around him."

"Who is he?" I asked again.

"Quinn," breathed Natalie. And while she might not be a fan of the Apathy Alliance, she did say his name with a certain amount of awe. "Quinn Riley."

"Okay," I said. "I'll be on the lookout for Quinn Riley."

"Oh —" said Natalie, startled by something else over my shoulder.

And at the same moment, a teasing male voice spoke close to my ear.

"No need to be on the lookout," the voice said. "Quinn Riley, at your service."

I didn't even have to turn around. I knew exactly whose gray-green eyes I'd see.

Sure enough, Quinn Riley and the Stairwell God were one and the same.

Eight

I did myself proud all over again, paralyzed brain and partially open mouth included. But this time I did manage to cough up some words. Well, one word. Here's what I said:

"Thanks."

Like he actually meant he was at my service, and like I was actually thanking him for it.

Then the bell rang, and Quinn Riley was gone, strolling away in what I soon learned was the signature gait of all Alliance members, though he did do it particularly well. The other kids parted before him like he was Moses and they were the Red Sea.

Left to my own devices, I probably would've sat there, staring at the door he'd walked through, until school shut down for the night. But Natalie was in my next class, too, and somehow she got me up and to the right classroom. At least, physically she did. My mind was in a different place entirely. I just kept replaying the same two scenes in my head on a continuous mental loop: first, Quinn and me in the stairwell, and second, Quinn and me in the lunchroom. And with each new playback, I had to mentally kick myself all over again.

There I'd been, practically face-to-face with the perfect guy — and I'd blown it, not just once but twice. It was like seeing that perfect wave rolling in, the type of wave most surfers only dream about. But instead of owning it, I'd let it wipe me out completely.

So I continued to obsess all the way through Modern Western Civilizations, and then some more as I drifted through precalculus. And the strangest part was that I don't usually obsess. I mean, nothing in Palo Alto had prepared me for such an immediate crush, much less for anybody like Quinn, but I'm mostly pretty good about picking myself up and moving on.

Either way, it wasn't until precalculus was nearly over and the mental playback/kicking myself count had reached double digits that the obsessing screeched to a halt and I finally had an epiphany. Suddenly, it all became perfectly clear.

The problem was much bigger than my pathetic reaction to an almost total stranger — it was my reaction to *everything* that had happened in the last week that was so wrong.

The cold ugly truth was that I'd been letting circumstances and chance own me. Which was the opposite of what my dad had taught me, and what my mother had taught me, too, though in a non-surfing way.

Ever since Thad and Nora told me the news, I'd been allowing other people to make my decisions. And the whole time, all

I'd been doing was feebly trying to explain that T.K. wasn't dead and waiting for something to change, or someone to come to the rescue.

When what I should have been doing was taking my destiny into my own hands. There was absolutely no reason why I shouldn't find my mother myself.

■　　■　　■

Last period was drama, but since it didn't start until the following week I had the hour free. And for the first time in days I knew exactly what I should do.

The Prescott library was on the top floor, stretching across both of the buildings that housed the school. I bypassed the shelves of books and rows of study carrels and made for a bank of computers along one wall.

I hadn't fully formulated a plan of attack, but I figured if I gathered as much information as I could about my mother's trip, I was bound to come up with some ideas. And it didn't take long to realize how little I knew about where she'd been going and what she'd intended to do. Patience wasn't the only sister whose name didn't fit — T.K. was involved in so many causes that it was hard to keep track, and she was pretty zealous about them all.

The obvious move would be to get in touch with Thad. He'd always insisted on knowing where T.K. was, in case anything urgent came up — he'd definitely have the itinerary for this last trip. He'd also probably have a good sense of what she was trying to accomplish, since T.K. had funded the excursion through TrueTech.org, the company's philanthropic arm.

But I was hoping that if I kept a low profile where Thad was concerned, he'd forget about the whole training-me-to-take-over-the-business thing. And given that he was the first person to insist that T.K. was dead, reaching out to him was far more likely to result in another lecture about denial than anything remotely helpful.

No, Thad was a nonstarter. But T.K. was enough of a public figure that there would be lots of information about her on the Internet, and some of it would have to be about recent events. So I pulled up a browser window and Googled T.K.'s name.

And while I knew my mother was pretty famous, at least in tech circles, nothing could have prepared me for what happened next.

On the screen was a long list of blue links, and each link led to an obituary.

I felt like all of the air had been sucked out of the room. The text went blurry, and there was a ringing noise in my ears. Without conscious direction, my hand reached out to the mouse, and the browser closed, but the images still seemed to linger on the screen.

No matter how confident a person is that she's right and everyone else is wrong, Google returning several hundred links that seem to agree with all the people who are wrong isn't the most comforting experience. If anything, it's the sort of experience that can make a person hyperventilate.

Which meant it was several minutes before I felt like I could breathe normally and face the computer again. But this time around I was more careful. I opened up a fresh browser window and went directly to TrueTech.org.

T.K. believes in keeping overhead low, and this was particularly true for the company's philanthropic activities — she always said she'd rather spend money on causes than fancy offices and staff. As a result, things like updating the Web site sometimes fell through the cracks, since nobody was paid to do it. And I was in luck — it looked like the site hadn't been touched since my mother left. There was a link right off the home page to a page that was all about the Antarctica excursion, like it hadn't even begun yet.

The stated objectives were to "Document the impact of global warming on Antarctic ice shelves and explore other environmental occurrences in the area," and the schedule called for the participants to meet up in Buenos Aires and catch a flight to Ushuaia, a port in Tierra del Fuego at the southernmost tip of Argentina. From there, they would board a small ship called the *Polar Star*, which was supposed to sail down and around the western side of the Antarctic continent, stopping every so often to do whatever tests they had planned and returning via New Zealand. The entire trip was scheduled to take nineteen days.

This was all still sort of vague, but at least I had more to work with. I made some notes in my otherwise-empty notebook, and then I went back to Google and typed in *Polar Star*. And that's when things got seriously weird.

According to the articles I found, the ship had sent its SOS signals on the morning of its seventh day out, from a point in the Amundsen Sea roughly between Thurston Island and Cape Dart. After that, it went radio silent. Meanwhile, the first rescuers arrived at the spot only an hour later and there was nothing at all to be seen, just like Thad said. The ship had vanished into thin air.

But it turned out that it wasn't easy for a ship to simply vanish, and especially not that quickly.

The general consensus was that the *Polar Star* must have hit submerged ice, which is what happened to a cruise ship called the *Explorer* in 2007. But the *Explorer* took nearly twenty hours to sink, which gave everyone on it plenty of time to evacuate by lifeboat. Even the *Titanic* had taken three hours to go down, which had been more than long enough to escape — there just weren't enough lifeboats for people like the guy played by Leonardo DiCaprio.

And I knew there was no way T.K. would've set foot on a boat without enough lifeboats. She wouldn't even release the parking brake on the Prius until everybody's seat belt was buckled.

So, given the lack of an actual sinking ship or lifeboats or anything, the hitting-ice-and-sinking theory seemed pretty weak.

I also found a lot of blog posts from people who had theories of their own. There was one guy who was convinced that T.K.'s ship had fallen prey to a band of marauding polar pirates. Another must have been watching too many old episodes of *The X-Files*, because he chalked it up to an alien abduction, an Antarctic version of the Bermuda Triangle, or some combination of the two.

These people might not be all that reliable, but a couple did point out something interesting. There are hundreds of satellites orbiting the earth, not just for beaming down TV to places that can't get cable but for taking pictures and measurements, too. Some of these satellites are dedicated to scientific research — observing changes in the earth's climate, for example. Others are used for less aboveboard activities, like spying on rogue nations' nuclear facilities and stalking celebrities.

Anyhow, according to the bloggers, there was a set of satellite images of the Amundsen Sea right before the *Polar Star* sent out its SOS signal, and the ship could be seen clearly, perfectly fine and sailing along without any problems. The next set of available satellite images for the area was from only a few minutes later, and the ship should still have been visible. But the *Polar Star* was completely gone — like it really had vanished into thin air. There wasn't any disturbance in the water to indicate a sinking ship, nor was there any smoke or debris from an explosion.

The bloggers used this as evidence to justify their random theories. Of course, they also believed in things like polar pirates and the Bermuda Triangle.

Still, I wanted to see those satellite images for myself, from the original sources. After all, ships don't just evaporate, complete with their crew and passengers and equipment and everything. Especially not when one of those passengers was my mother.

And I couldn't be the only person who thought there had to be more to this story than we'd been told.

Nine

Charley had texted earlier, offering to come pick me up, but I was sort of fascinated by the subway and told her I'd be fine getting back to the loft on my own. She replied with several texts' worth of instructions about which station was most convenient to Prescott, how to buy a MetroCard, which line to take, how to behave on the subway platform and in the train so that people wouldn't think I was a tourist, which stop to get off at, and the best route from there to the loft. If I hadn't realized that she was still overcompensating for the airport mix-up, I would've worried that she didn't think I was very bright.

Anyhow, when the final bell rang, I was ready to go. I collected my things, checked Charley's instructions again, and dashed to the nearest subway station. The entrance was exactly where Charley had said it would be, and it wasn't hard to buy a MetroCard or figure out which train was the right one.

As it rattled through the tunnel, I felt buoyant, like I was floating instead of underground. I couldn't wait to tell Charley everything I'd learned about the *Polar Star* and get her thoughts about what to do next. And even in my excitement — after all, the evidence I'd found clearly suggested that T.K.'s ship hadn't gone down, at least not the way everyone said it did, which could only be good news — I couldn't help but think that Charley would probably have some helpful ideas about Quinn, too. She was gorgeous and confident and she definitely had far more experience than I did in these matters — just about anyone did.

The subway was amazingly fast, and it was also a lot less stressful than the ride uptown with Patience had been. Half an hour after I'd left Prescott I was back at the loft.

I found Charley sprawled on a sofa. They'd finished filming the night I'd arrived, so now, at Dieter's insistence, she was reading a book titled *The Theory of Meta-Surrealism in Neo-Industrial Film: Post-Production as Praxis.* Dieter said it would be impossible to begin the editing process until everyone involved had finished "zis mastervork," as it had inspired his artistic vision. Charley seemed to be finding it less inspiring.

"Oh thank God," she said when she saw me, slamming the book shut and practically leaping up from the sofa. "I'm so glad you're here. You have to tell me all about your day. I want to know everything, from the second you got there to the second you left, and not just because I'll poke my eyes out if I have to slog through any more of this book. And I think we should do it over ice cream. But I need to go get some, which means you have to chaperone me so I don't buy out the entire store. I have absolutely no willpower when it comes to ice cream. Want to run to the deli with me?"

"Sure," I said, but just then her phone started to ring. She checked the screen and frowned.

"I should get this," she said apologetically.

"I can go," I said.

"Are you sure? Do you know where it is? Do you need money?"

"I'm all set. What flavor do you want?"

"Chocolate anything is good. And don't let me eat more than half a pint by myself. Or maybe three-quarters if I behave myself and ask very nicely."

■　■　■

There was a deli on the corner, and I carefully selected a pint of chocolate peanut butter and another of chocolate chip cookie dough from the freezer section. And then, after a little more careful thought, I added a pint of java mocha fudge.

The guy at the counter looked from me to the ice cream and back again. "You are relative of lady down the street?" he asked. It wasn't clear whether he figured this out based on my appearance or my selections, but apparently Charley was a regular visitor to his freezer section.

I had a full set of keys by then, including one for the elevator, but I took the stairs to justify the java mocha fudge. I figured the climb to the fifth floor was worth at least a quarter-pint and maybe more, since carrying the ice cream was sort of like carrying hand weights.

While the elevator opened directly into the apartment, announcing its arrival with a beep, the entrance from the stairs didn't have that feature, so Charley didn't hear me come in. And while she'd taken the phone into her bedroom, she hadn't shut her door, and the loft had the acoustics of a concert hall. Which meant her side of the conversation sounded as clear as if she were standing right next to me.

"The poor kid's already had to adjust to a lot in a short period of time," she was saying in an aggravated way. "And I think she's making good progress. There's no need to rush things."

There was a long pause, which gave me every opportunity to make some noise and let Charley know I was back, but it was impossible not to want to listen in. I mean, I didn't know what 'poor kid' she'd be talking about besides me and, judging by her tone, it was probably Patience on the other end of the line.

"I wouldn't describe it as a fantasy," said Charley. "More an understandable reluctance to meet reality head-on —"

Patience, if it was Patience, must have interrupted her then, because there was another pause before Charley spoke again, and when she did, she sounded even more aggravated than she had before.

"As usual, you're completely overreacting," she said. "She hasn't said a word about it since right after she got here. I knew I shouldn't have told you. You're blowing it all out of proportion. There's no need to take such drastic measures."

There was yet another pause, and when Charley spoke next, it sounded like her teeth were clenched from the effort it took to control her temper.

"I'll tell you what. I'll feel her out over the weekend. If she still seems to be having difficulty coming to terms with everything, then I'll take her to see someone. Will that satisfy you?"

Patience — and by now I was positive it was Patience, because who else could it be? — must have eventually agreed, because the topic changed to logistics for the weekend in Southampton. But I was no longer paying attention.

I knew it was wrong to listen in on private conversations, but I was glad I'd heard what I'd heard. Because there was no way I could ask Charley for help now.

In fact, I shouldn't even have let her know I still thought T.K. was alive, and I definitely shouldn't tell her anything about my search for her. It would only lead to daily sessions with a child psychiatrist or something like that. And it sounded like Patience was all ready to haul me off to whichever insane asylum was the mental institution of choice for the offspring of New York's power and social elite.

The truth was, if I were my aunts, I'd probably be thinking along the same lines. To them, I must seem as deluded as the alien abduction and polar pirate people.

But I wasn't deluded. I couldn't explain it, not rationally, but that didn't mean I couldn't *feel* it. And I did feel it — with every atom in my body.

I didn't care what everyone else thought.

T.K. was still alive. She had to be. And I knew I'd find her.

But it looked like I was going to have to do it on my own.

Ten

I opened and shut the door to the loft again, this time with a gentle slam, and Charley's voice softened to a murmur. A moment later, she emerged from her bedroom, looking so worry-free that I almost wondered if I'd misunderstood her end of the conversation. But I didn't know how else to interpret what I'd heard.

Regardless of what she might be thinking about my mental state, Charley definitely approved of my taste in ice cream. She scooped big helpings into bowls for us both, and then she insisted on a detailed account of my day. So I tried to look as worry-free as she did as I told her all about Mr. Seton and Natalie and the welcome I'd received from the Flying Monkeys. And while I carefully excised any mention of static-filled messages from unknown numbers, epiphanies, or satellite photos, I did tell her about Quinn — not that there was much to tell.

Charley still found it incredibly exciting, and she wanted to role-play what I should say when I saw him next. "Guys love talking about themselves," she said, spooning out more java mocha fudge. "What is Quinn into?"

"Did you miss the part where I completely choked in his presence? Besides, according to Natalie, he's not into anything," I said. And I explained about the Apathy Alliance.

"He's a teenage boy — they're every bit as insecure as teenage girls, and usually more so. The apathy thing is probably just an act."

"Maybe," I said, but I wasn't so sure.

Over the next few days, I did catch the occasional glimpse of Quinn at school, but I didn't get a chance to try out any of Charley's suggestions. Every time I saw him, he was holding court on the stairwell landing, and the Alliance minions around him functioned like a human force field.

Meanwhile, I was spending every free moment scouring the Web for information about T.K. and the *Polar Star*, but I didn't come up with anything new. I'd e-mailed the bloggers who'd posted the satellite photos, but I hadn't heard back, and "Out of Area" didn't call again. The only other messages I got were from Erin and Justin. And, of course, from Charley, who was determined to do the entire guardian thing right and make up for any early missteps.

This mostly meant including vegetables in whatever we ordered in, since she'd quickly abandoned any pretense of knowing how to cook, and a single attempt to help with my homework made it painfully obvious that she was just as clueless as I was when it came to science.

And that wasn't the only thing we had in common. We liked the same magazines and music and TV shows. We even used the same brand of toothpaste and drank the same kind of soda. By Friday, it felt like I'd known Charley my whole life, and like there'd never been a time when we hadn't eaten takeout together while watching teen movie classics, which was rapidly becoming our standard dinner routine. She did go out one night with a Swedish guy named Lars, but otherwise evenings were as tame as they'd been at home.

Either way, it was a relief when the weekend finally rolled around. Even if you didn't plan on staying long, starting a new school wasn't the least stressful thing. And even if two days with Patience, her husband, and the Flying Monkeys wasn't what I'd choose if I had any choice, I was looking forward to sand and ocean.

According to Charley, that was just about all I could look forward to. As soon as I got home from school on Friday, we set out for my grandparents' house in Southampton. My grandparents wouldn't actually be there — they spent most of their time in Palm Beach — but from what Charley had told me, I wouldn't be missing much.

"I still think I was adopted," she said from behind the wheel of her Mini Cooper. She drove well but way too fast, and she took special joy in cutting off drivers of big SUVs, considering it part of her personal effort to lower carbon emissions. She had that in common with T.K., if nothing else.

"Reggie — his full name is Reginald Phineas Baxter Truesdale, and he's even the Fifth, if you can believe it, because who wouldn't want to keep a name like that going — anyhow, he's not the most spontaneous guy," said Charley. "When the weather's good, he plays golf at his club in the country. When the weather's bad, he plays squash and backgammon at his club in the city. And no matter what the weather's like, he drinks a lot of scotch."

My grandmother didn't sound any better. "You know the phrase 'nature abhors a vacuum'?" Charley asked. "Well, Adele Kittredge Truesdale abhors a vacuum, too. Since Reggie hardly talks, Old Addie has to fill the void." I didn't think Charley would appreciate my pointing out that Old Addie seemed to have passed this trait along to her youngest daughter since it argued against her whole adoption theory.

Anyhow, it turned out that New Yorkers' idea of the beach was actually most people's idea of a suburb near the ocean. The town of Southampton had a lot of upscale boutiques and cafes, but once we passed through the commercial district we ended up in a neighborhood of tree-lined streets and shingled houses. Only the faint taste of salt in the air hinted at the Atlantic nearby.

As Charley drove on, the trees shading the streets began to get taller and the houses started getting bigger and fancier. Then you couldn't tell anymore since high green hedges started hiding the houses from view. Finally, at the very end of a dead-end street, she swung the car through a gate that was almost hidden in the highest set of hedges yet. "Home sweet home," she announced. "At least, one of them."

A long gravel drive stretched before us, curving into a wide loop in front of the house. But calling it a house would be like calling Godzilla a sweet little gecko. The design was traditional — silvery-gray shingles with white-painted gables — but it was the size of a city block.

There's a crazy amount of Internet money in Silicon Valley, and a few of the tech billionaires have gone sort of nutty finding ways to spend it, but most people are pretty understated. There are a lot more hybrids than Ferraris, and the same aesthetic tends to apply to houses.

This, on the other hand, was totally out of sync with "less is more." I'd known the Truesdales were wealthy, but it was still way beyond what I'd expected.

"Cozy, isn't it?" said Charley. "Wait until you see the place in Florida. It has a fountain. With cherubs."

"How —?" I started to ask. But even T.K., who believes that every question deserves an answer, doesn't think it's polite to talk about money.

Charley must have guessed what I wanted to know. "It all goes back to the first Reginald Phineas Baxter Truesdale."

"What did he do?" I asked.

Charley parked the car to one side of the drive, slipping it into a narrow slot between a Mercedes and a BMW. "You really want to know?" she asked. "Most Truesdales don't like to be reminded of the roots of the great Truesdale fortune."

"Why? Was he a slave dealer or a bootlegger or something like that? Or — oh my God, was he in the Mafia?"

She laughed. "That would definitely explain a lot about Patty. No, Reggie One was a coal tycoon in the nineteenth century. He pioneered new ways of strip mining — you know, when you slice off the top of a mountain to get at the coal, rather than going to all the trouble of digging for it? And while he was at it, he also pioneered new ways of abusing his workers."

"Oh," I said, digesting this as we retrieved our overnight bags from the car. "That sounds sort of evil."

She gave a wry smile. "We're descended from a long line of evil people."

Suddenly, T.K.'s passion for all of her causes made sense like it never had before. I mean, there's nothing wrong with trying to help people and save the planet and everything, obviously, but she did get carried away sometimes. Now I wondered if she was also trying to atone for her family's past.

A man in a white shirt and dark trousers met us at the front door. At first I thought he was Patience's husband, but his name was Frederick, and he was sort of like a butler. He offered to show me to my room, but Charley thanked him and said she'd take care of it herself.

She led me up a polished staircase and down a long hallway. Everything was carefully informal, with lots of cotton fabrics and wicker, but it still managed to look fabulously expensive. "Frederick would've put you in a guest room at the other end of the house, but I want you close by for moral support," said Charley.

"Will I need moral support?" I asked.

"You'll be fine. I'm the one who'll need help. Now, I thought you might want to stay in your mom's old room. But only if you want to."

She tried to say this casually, but I could tell she was worried that mentioning my mother might upset me. And I wasn't sure how to play it. How was I supposed to react if I'd "come to terms with everything" and didn't still think T.K. was alive? Like her room would make me sad? Or like I'd want to stay there, because it would be a point of connection?

"Um, I guess that sounds good," I said, deciding to go with ambivalent, which was easy since it was close to what I actually felt.

The room was a couple of doors down from Charley's, and she seemed relieved when I didn't burst into tears on the threshold. "We have fifteen minutes or so to get settled before dinner," she told me. "I can come get you when it's time to go downstairs. Or maybe you should come get me? I don't think I can handle another lecture on punctuality from Patty, and you're much better at it than I am." This was true, but only because just about anybody had to be more punctual than Charley.

After she left, I set my bag on a low upholstered bench next to the window, which looked out on the beach and the ocean beyond. The sun was just starting to set, and the light was all gold and glimmery on the water. It was hard to believe that less than a week ago I'd been at Ross's Cove, at the exact same time of day but on the opposite coast.

I didn't have much to unpack, so I spent the time exploring T.K.'s room. Somebody — and I knew it couldn't have been my mother — had decorated the room in pastels and chintz, but it was still as uncluttered and impersonal as a hotel, like anything that had ever belonged to T.K. had been packed away. The only thing I knew for sure was hers was a stack of Outward Bound brochures I found in a desk drawer.

T.K. had gone on a bunch of Outward Bound programs when she was younger. She'd liked them so much that she'd been threatening to send me for years, describing it as "an important opportunity to acquire self-sufficiency." I knew I could always fake appendicitis and get myself medevaced out if she insisted on packing me off to the wilderness, but fortunately it never came to that.

I'd mostly blocked out her rapturous descriptions — I mean, could using leaves as toilet paper really be such a thrill? — but flipping through the brochures reminded me of something: One of her trips had been a six-week camping excursion in Alaska. The brochure for it was right there in the stack with the others.

It read like the script for a horror movie, but I found all of the breathless guarantees about teaching Arctic survival skills ("Learn to identify edible lichen!") strangely comforting.

■　■　■

Dinner was served precisely at half past seven in the dining room. This was the first I'd seen of Patience, Jeremy, and the twins since we'd arrived, but the house was so big it was possible they had their own wing.

According to Charley, Patience and Jeremy had met in law school and immediately recognized each other as soul mates. They even worked together, doing something complicated in the intersection of law and finance.

Jeremy looked just as blond and highly strung as Patience, but they were both nice enough at dinner. Jeremy was on the quiet side, which might explain how Grey came by his own conversational grace, but Patience asked me lots of questions about school and my impressions of New York so far.

She didn't eat much, so she had plenty of time to talk, but it was more like she was trying to make me feel at home. Maybe to her, convening this family weekend was part of fulfilling her responsibilities. And I had to admit, I kind of admired her no-nonsense directness, though I could see how it might be an annoying quality in a sibling. She said what she thought, without trying to sugarcoat it or hide her motives, and she was usually on target even if she wasn't tactful.

Gwyneth and Grey were nice enough, too, if by nice enough you mean speaking when spoken to with as little animation as a person could have without being in a coma. I was next to Gwyneth, and by accident I'd reached for her water glass when we first sat down. As a result, I learned the hard way that what looked like water was actually straight vodka. Judging by how Grey sipped from his own water glass, I had a feeling it'd been filled from the same bottle.

"Delia, who is this Thaddeus J. Wilcox person?" Patience asked over the raspberry sorbet we had for dessert.

"Thad? He's like my mother's right-hand guy at TrueTech," I said.

"I've been trying to reach him all week and he hasn't returned any of my calls. You do own the majority of TrueTech's shares now, and it's never too early to start laying the foundation for the future. Temperance was quite explicit about this Thad person taking the lead on training you. I'm surprised by his lack of follow-up."

I was even more surprised than she was. Thad was big on follow-up, and I knew that keeping a low profile wouldn't keep me safe for long. But it turned out I hadn't been keeping a low profile, because Patience had been calling to remind him about me. It didn't make any sense. "He's probably been swamped without my mother there," I said, adding a silent prayer that he would stay swamped indefinitely.

Patience looked like she wanted to pursue this topic further, but Gwyneth, who'd polished off the contents of her water glass between the Chilean sea bass and the sorbet, broke in at just the right moment. "May we be excused?" she asked.

"It depends," said Patience. "What are you planning on doing?"

"A friend's having some people over," she said.

"Which friend?" asked Jeremy.

"Quinn Riley," said Gwyneth. "And yes, his parents will be there and no, there won't be any drinking or illegal activities of any kind." I could see that her fingers were crossed under the table, but this only registered dimly through the small spasm of brain paralysis caused by the mention of Quinn's name.

"Oh, then that's fine," said Patience. "In fact, why don't you take Delia with you? It would be good for her to get to know some of the other boys and girls from the right families." Then she added, turning to me, "And Quinn's father runs a very successful hedge fund. Energy investments, mostly, but he may do some high-tech. Connections are very important in the business world, and you're never too young to start making them."

"Is that Hunter Riley?" asked Charley. She'd been on her best behavior all through dinner, though I could tell she'd secretly been counting how many times Patience had used the word "appropriate." But now there was a strange edge to her voice.

"Uh-huh," said Grey, thus doubling his contribution to the evening's discourse. He'd also said "thanks" when his mother had handed him the salt.

Charley looked at me like there was more to what she was saying than the words themselves. "Delia, I didn't realize — I didn't put the names together. You don't have to go if you don't want to."

Patience gave an impatient shake of her head. "Don't be ridiculous, Charity. That was all ages ago. Delia, go with Gwyneth and Grey and have a good time."

I should have been torn. If I was trying to prove how well I was adjusting, then it seemed like I should go. But Charley clearly had something against Quinn's father. With the exception of her blood relatives and Helga, Charley liked everyone, so this was weird.

But I'd also been spending a lot of time thinking about what I'd say to Quinn when I saw him next. I'd even sunk to a whole new level of pathetic by practicing in front of the bathroom mirror. So I wasn't about to pass up an opportunity to offset my previous stunning displays of idiocy.

"I'll go for a little while, I guess," I said, trying to sound mildly reluctant for Charley's sake.

"Okay. But promise to call if you want to come home and

the twins aren't ready to leave yet," she said, the edge still in her voice.

"I'm sure the kids can get there and back on their own," said Patience. "They won't even have to drive. The Rileys bought the old Aronson house a few years ago. They're just up the beach."

Eleven

I followed my cousins through a set of French doors and out onto the lawn. Summer was almost over, and the air was cooler now that the sun had set, but it still felt comfortable without a jacket or sweater. We skirted a tennis court and a pool before reaching the steep wooden stairs that led down to the beach.

"Thanks for not saying anything," said Gwyneth at the bottom of the stairs.

"About what?" I asked.

"About the water glass."

"Oh. No problem."

"I can show you where they keep the liquor," she offered.

I probably should've been touched, and maybe even flattered, but I was too distracted. I mean, I would've already had enough on my mind, between prepping for a Quinn encounter and worrying about whether my purple Calypso dress really worked with my silver ballet flats — or if it mattered, since there was a good chance nobody would notice me with my willowy blond cousin around. But now I was also wondering about Charley's bizarre reaction to Hunter Riley's name.

The Rileys' house was only a few minutes' walk up the beach, and while it wasn't as big as my grandparents' house, it was still huge. And Quinn's idea of "having some people over" turned out to include at least fifty people at the pool and another fifty on a deck above — not that Quinn was anywhere in sight. Music blasted from hidden speakers, so loud that the deck vibrated with the thump of the bass line.

Grey immediately disappeared, and I let Gwyneth lead me over to a clump of kids. She introduced me around, but it was so noisy that it was hard to catch anybody's name. Nobody seemed very interested in talking anyway. Mostly people just stood there, sipping drinks from plastic cups.

Half an hour later, I still hadn't seen any sign of Quinn, and the nervous anticipation from the walk over was starting to evaporate. When I caught myself stifling a yawn, I even started to worry that apathy was contagious and began calculating how much longer I'd have to stay. And at just that moment, someone tapped me on the arm.

A surge of excited panic shot through me, but I told myself to stay calm, smile, and otherwise act like someone whose brain actually functioned. Then I turned around.

But it was only Natalie. "Hi," she said. Her own smile was so friendly that I almost felt guilty about how disappointed I was to see her and not Quinn.

"What happened?" a guy I'd recognized from Prescott asked her. "Did they cancel SAT prep tonight?"

"Oh, no. That class is only on Tuesdays and Thursdays," said Natalie, her green eyes innocent. "Sometimes they do extra sessions on Saturday mornings, but not until later in the school year." Her delivery was so smooth that it took him a second to realize she was mocking him right back.

He sidled away, and Natalie drew me aside. "I'm so glad to see someone *normal* here," she confided. "I hate parties. I try to avoid them when I can. The only reason I'm even here is that my college application coach thinks social skills are an important differentiator to admissions officers, so my mom and dad make me practice."

I wasn't sure what to say to that, but something buzzing in Natalie's handbag saved me from answering. She dug out an iPhone and checked the screen. "Figures. It's my parents, making sure that I'm actually here instead of at the library, like last time. Sorry — this will be quick."

I waited for a bit, but when I realized that her parents were quizzing her on every conversation she'd had so far, I signaled that I'd be back in a few minutes. She flashed me an apologetic look, and I escaped into the house.

There were a ton of people inside, too, but all I wanted just then was solitude. The evening was turning into a total bust. The worst part was that it was still too early to leave, at least if I was trying to prove how well-adjusted I was.

I wandered through the house, eventually finding a deserted sitting room as far away from the party as I could get. Everything was sleek and modern, with a lot of glass and chrome, but in its own way it was just as impersonal as my grandparents' house. I sank into a chair upholstered in soft dark leather and picked up one of the enormous books on the coffee table, a collection of black-and-white photographs of sharecroppers during the Great Depression. The photos were pretty grim, with face after face staring out bleakly from the pages, but they sort of suited my mood.

As I sat there, the sounds from the party were like a muted soundtrack, the music and the voices blurring together in a low rumble of noise. But after a bit, one of the voices separated itself from the others, and I realized it was coming from an entirely different direction. At first I thought it was a TV, because the voice kept rising and falling like an actor's does when he's playing a part. Then I began to make out specific words: Muggle, Hermione, Hedwig, Slytherin.

Somebody nearby was reading aloud from *Harry Potter*. Which was pretty much the last thing I expected. Especially given that the other reading material available in the house seemed like it had been chosen mostly to match the decor.

I put the book of photos back on the coffee table and followed the voice through another empty room and down a dim hallway. At the end of the hallway, a sliver of yellow light spilled from a partially open door. I could hear the voice clearly now, on the other side of the door, and I knew exactly whose voice it was.

But I still couldn't figure out why Quinn was hiding out from his own party, not to mention reading out loud while he hid.

My first instinct was to go say hello. In theory, it would be the perfect opportunity to show him I was capable of coherent speech. But I felt funny about it. After all, if he wanted to see people, he wouldn't be hanging out at the complete other end of the house, would he?

So even though I'd promised myself that I was taking charge of my own destiny, I turned around and quietly returned the way I'd come.

■ ■ ■

Outside, the party hadn't gotten any less crowded or loud. If anything, it was gathering strength. Somebody had started a drinking game involving croquet mallets and tequila shots, and somebody else had started a drinking game involving badminton racquets and empty beer cans. I didn't see Grey anywhere, but I was just in time to spot Gwyneth heading toward the beach with one of the guys she'd been talking to before.

"There you are," said Natalie, coming up beside me. "I was thinking of organizing a search-and-rescue mission."

"What?" I asked, startled. Of course, Natalie had no way of knowing how much time I'd been spending lately thinking about the same thing.

"A search-and-rescue mission. You know, like when hikers don't come back or a plane goes down or a ship sinks —" She stopped short, and a look of horror spread across her face. "Oh. Oh, no. I'm sorry. I wasn't thinking."

"It's okay."

"See, this is why I need to practice my social skills. I'm always saying the wrong thing."

"Really, it's fine."

"Do you — do you want to talk about it?" she asked gingerly.

I had to laugh. She was trying not to wince, but she wasn't doing a very good job. When I'd first met Natalie, she'd reminded me of Erin and Justin. Now she reminded me of T.K., who would rather shave her head than talk about feelings.

"No," I told her. "All I want is to find my mother."

"But — you mean, you think she's still alive?"

I nodded. "I know she is."

"What makes you think so?" she asked.

I examined her expression carefully. If she thought I was crazy, she was hiding it better than she'd hid the wince, and she sounded genuinely curious.

So I told her everything. After all, it wasn't like Natalie was tight with Patience or Charley or my cousins — I didn't have to worry that she'd give me away. I even told her about the bloggers and the sixteen-second voice mail. It was a relief to get it all out.

She didn't skip a beat. "Have you tried to trace the voice mail? Assuming it was a wireless call, whoever initiated it had to be in range of a site base station, and the signal would be transmitted from there to the nearest landline network for transfer to the fiber backbone, where it would bounce from point to point before being relayed to the tower that ultimately delivered the data stream to your handset, leaving a record throughout the switching system. You just need to know how to access it."

I'd been lost pretty much since she asked if I'd traced the call. So I just focused on the last thing she'd said. "Do you know how to access it?" I asked. "The switching backbone thingie?"

"I could try to hack into it."

"Really?"

"Sure. It shouldn't be hard. I'll just need to download some data from your phone."

She was completely serious. And if it meant tracing the call, I was happy to give her all the data she wanted. I'd even be happy to practice social skills with her.

Twelve

We both agreed that we'd put in enough time at the party to please her parents and my aunts, so we went around to the street out front, where Natalie had parked her car. Most people keep CDs and maps and stuff like that in their glove compartments, but she pulled a memory stick out of hers and used it to transfer the data she needed from my phone.

"I like doing this kind of thing," she said, waving away my thanks like I was the one doing her a favor. "It's fun. And I'll let you know as soon as I figure anything out." I thought she had strange ideas about fun, but I wasn't going to complain.

She dropped me off on her own way home, and Charley appeared as soon as I let myself in through the massive front door. "Well?" she asked, dragging me into the kitchen and pulling a carton of brownie caramel crunch from an industrial-sized freezer. "How was it?"

Given how she'd acted at dinner, I was worried that the only reason she'd waited up was to warn me off Quinn, but when I told her how little I'd accomplished on that front, she seemed nearly as disappointed as I was. And she didn't know what to make of *Harry Potter*, either.

"But look on the bright side," she said. "At least he wasn't drunk and hitting on every girl in sight."

"Is that what his father's like? Hunter? Is that why you don't like him?" I asked.

"Who told you I don't like Hunter Riley?" she asked.

"You did, at dinner. Maybe not in those exact words, but you made it sort of obvious how you felt."

She started to protest, but she gave it up pretty quickly. "You're right," she admitted. "I don't like him. And I didn't realize when you were talking about Quinn that he was Hunter's son."

"So what's so awful about Hunter Riley?"

"You really want to know?"

"Is it worse than finding out that my ancestors were mountain-destroying labor exploiters?"

"That's good," she said, impressed. "I've never heard it put so succinctly."

"I'm waiting," I reminded her.

She sighed and put down her spoon. "The reason I don't like Hunter is because he completely destroyed the life of Quinn's mother, Paula, who also happened to be a friend of mine, because sometimes the world is just too small."

"How did he destroy her life?"

"For one, he started fooling around while they were still married, and he didn't even try to be subtle about it. Then, about ten years ago, when their marriage officially hit the rocks and they were getting divorced, he sued her for custody of their kid."

"Their kid being Quinn?"

"Their kid being Quinn," she agreed.

"The cheating thing was bad, but what was so wrong with wanting custody?"

"Hunter completely smeared Paula to get it. He'd made a fortune with his hedge fund — even with the whole financial crisis he's still been raking it in — and he hired the sharkiest, most expensive lawyers in town to rip her to shreds. They ended up having a very nasty, very public custody battle, during which he said she was mentally unstable and an unfit mother and a lot of other things that you don't exactly want being said about you all over Page Six."

I did the math. "So Quinn was what — seven or eight when this happened?"

"Something like that, which brings me to the worst part. Hunter got Quinn to testify against his mother."

"How? I mean, what could a seven-year-old have to say?"

"Whatever his father told him to say, I imagine."

"That must have been awful." I was thinking of Quinn, but Charley assumed I was talking about Paula.

"She was absolutely devastated. After she lost the custody battle, she moved to the West Coast, to Los Angeles or Seattle or someplace like that. I haven't heard from her since."

She picked up the now-empty carton of ice cream and moved

to throw it away, but then she hesitated, like she wasn't sure whether she should say what she was about to say.

"What?" I asked.

"It's just — I know it's none of my business, and it's all ancient history, and I'm the last person to blame the son for the sins of the father, especially given the Reggies, and this isn't to say that Quinn isn't a wonderful guy, but now that we both know more about him — ugh, I don't know how to say this."

I'd never heard her sound so awkward. "Say what, already?" I asked.

"I guess what I'm trying to say is proceed with caution. Okay?"

She looked at me intently. "Okay," I said. "But, just to keep things in perspective, he's said two sentences to me and I've said one word to him. I don't think he even knows my name. So I don't know how much caution I really need."

This made her laugh. "Well, it never hurts to be prepared."

■　　■　　■

I forgot to close the curtains, so I was up soon after dawn the next morning. The sky was hazy, like it couldn't decide what kind of day it wanted to become, but the sun glowed brightly enough through the haze to fill the room with light.

I could hear the waves rolling up onto the sand, and from the window I could even make out a distant figure with a surfboard. I hurriedly put on my bathing suit and an old shirt of my dad's that I used as a cover-up and headed downstairs. Then I let myself out through the same French doors as the night before and took the same path down to the beach, leaving my flip-flops at the bottom of the stairs.

Almost without thinking, I turned in the direction of the surfer I'd seen through the window. Since I didn't have my board, I couldn't surf myself, but at least I could get a vicarious thrill from watching somebody else. But once I got closer, I realized that the lone surfer in the distance was actually a guy with two young kids, and he was teaching them how to surf.

I took off my cover-up, spread it on the sand, and sat down to watch. They were far enough away that I couldn't hear more than the occasional cry of success, but I could see when one of the kids managed to stay upright on the board for a second or two, and I found myself smiling whenever that happened. I knew exactly how those first fleeting moments felt, and the kids' instructor cheering them on reminded me of my dad when he was teaching me.

It's not like I avoid thinking about my dad, but I try not to do it too much. For the first couple of years after he died, seeing or hearing something that unexpectedly triggered a memory could make me miss him so much it physically hurt.

That still happened sometimes, but there was something about this specific memory that wasn't painful — just purely sweet. When I closed my eyes, it was almost as good as if he'd been sitting next to me.

It was maybe a couple of minutes after that when the kids started shrieking.

Before I even had time to think, I was up and running. By the time I reached them, they'd dashed up onto the beach, so at least I knew they weren't drowning, but they were screaming and pointing at something in the water.

"What's wrong?" I panted to the kids, a boy and a girl in matching wet suits.

But as soon as I saw what they were pointing at, I figured out the problem. An enormous jellyfish bobbed lazily in the water, while farther out their instructor was paddling the surfboard toward shore. The haze had burned off and the sun was low in the sky behind him, so all I could see was his silhouette, but it was still clear that he was on a collision course with the pinkish blob.

The kids' words came out in a babbled, overlapping rush:

"The board got away from us —"

"And the undertow washed it really far out —"

"And he swam to get it —"

"And then we saw the jellyfish —"

"So we ran —"

"But what if it stings him —"

"He can't hear us —"

"On the count of three," I said. "We all yell 'jellyfish' as loud as we can, okay?"

I counted to three and we yelled, but the guy paddling the board just cupped an ear with his hand and shook his head. Between the surf and the wind, we couldn't make ourselves understood.

It's not like it was a shark, and jellyfish stings aren't exactly fatal — at least, most aren't — but they can still be pretty dangerous, especially if the person getting stung turns out to be allergic. And this jellyfish was seriously huge.

Before I could talk myself out of doing anything stupid, I grabbed a stick of driftwood from the beach and rushed into the water. I didn't have a specific plan — everything happened in a lot less time than it takes to describe it — mostly I was just hoping that the stick was longer than the jellyfish's tentacles.

The surf had picked up, and I ducked under one wave and then another, keeping my eye on the big blob rocking to and fro as the water pulled it along. I stopped about six or seven feet away, treading water with my legs and one arm while stretching my other arm out as far as it would go to extending the stick toward the jellyfish. I held my breath as it made contact.

Beneath the water's surface, there was a flash of movement as the tentacles lashed out in response to the foreign touch, and my body instinctively flinched. But I lodged the stick's end against the jellyfish and started pushing it down the shore, kicking my legs as hard as I could to keep the undertow from dragging us both closer to the guy on the surfboard.

Out of the corner of my eye, I saw a blur that was him approaching, and I heard someone say, "Delia?" But I kept kicking and pushing with the stick, concentrating on maneuvering the jellyfish out of his path and trying not to think about the way my heart was pounding.

And at just the right moment, another wave came along, larger than the others. I gave a final, fierce push with my stick. The water carried the jellyfish away and safely out of striking range.

I was relieved, but the relief was nothing compared to the euphoria.

And the euphoria had nothing to do with the jellyfish. I'd practically forgotten about the jellyfish already.

I hadn't been able to make out his features before, when he'd been nothing but a moving shape outlined by the sun. But I'd recognized him immediately when he spoke. Hearing him before actually seeing him was getting to be sort of a pattern.

More importantly, Quinn had recognized me, too.

And it turned out that he knew my name after all.

Thirteen

The kids were named Bea and Oliver, and Quinn wasn't just their surf instructor, he was also their brother. Which probably meant he hadn't been reading aloud to himself the night before — he'd had an audience. And he hadn't been hiding out, either — he'd been putting Bea and Oliver to bed.

So that was a lot less strange. If anything, it was sort of sweet, and not at all what I'd expected. The elusive, teasing guy from school with the crew of Alliance followers didn't compute with the *Harry Potter*–reading big brother.

The kids had jumped on Quinn as soon as we reached the beach, and they made a fuss over me, too. I tried to protest that it wasn't a big deal, but they were having none of it.

"It was a gigantic deal," insisted Bea. "You saved Quinn's life."

"Now you're responsible for him until he saves your life back," said Oliver.

"Is that how it works?" Quinn asked, amused.

"It might be the other way around," said Bea. "I can't remember."

Just then a woman appeared at the top of a path leading up

from the dunes, and I realized that we were practically in front of the Rileys' house. "Beatrice! Oliver!" she called. She was wearing yoga clothes and big dark sunglasses, and it looked like she had her highlights done at the same place as Patience. "Time to come in. You have tennis, and then the Castelli children will be here for a playdate."

"Ugh," said Bea. "I hate, hate, hate tennis. Hate it."

"And Ashley Castelli picks her nose," said Oliver.

"The Castelli children are very nice," the woman said. "And one day you'll be glad you've had all these tennis lessons."

"Which day?" asked Oliver.

Her sigh was audible even from a distance. "Quinn, will you send them up here, please?"

The looks Bea and Oliver gave Quinn were heart-wrenching, but Quinn shook his head. "Sorry, guys. It's not up to me. You'd better go."

They trudged off like they'd just received a life sentence in one of those Iraqi prisons, but I got a hug from Bea first, and Oliver bumped his fist against mine.

"Oh, and Quinn," said the woman as she shunted the kids toward the house, "your father would like to see you. He should be home from his workout soon."

"Okay," he called back, making no move to follow Bea and Oliver. He turned to me and shrugged. "Stepmother," he said, as if that said it all.

"Is your dad angry about the party last night?"

"Were you there?" he asked, surprised. "I didn't see you."

"Just for a little while," I hedged. It wasn't like I was going to admit that I'd been pretty much stalking him. "My cousins brought me."

"Oh, right," he said, and the way he said it almost made me wonder if he'd asked around about me. How else could he know my name and who my cousins were? But someone like him must have better things to do. "No, I don't think he and Fiona — my stepmom — even realize anyone was here, and Bea and Oliver won't rat me out. Besides, my dad can wait. These waves are too good to pass up. Do you surf?"

My heart gave a little skip. I didn't think I was imagining the note of invitation in his voice, but I couldn't be sure. "Uh-huh. But my board's at home, in California."

"I've got an extra if you're up for it."

When he looked at me with those gray-green eyes, he could've been asking if I was up for hunting down that jellyfish and eating it for lunch. Either way, I would've said yes.

■　　■　　■

Quinn's extra board was from when he was younger, so it wasn't too long for me, and the water was warm enough that I was fine without a wet suit, though I was feeling a bit exposed in my one-piece. But I forgot about that as soon as I was back in the water. And while the surfing was great, the best part was that between the jellyfish drama and meeting Bea and Oliver and everything, the brain paralysis hadn't had a chance to kick in — I was actually acting like a normal person for once, or at least mostly normal.

We'd been out there for about an hour when I started thinking I should probably get back. Charley didn't know where I was, and while I didn't want to go, I also didn't want her to worry.

"I'll walk you," offered Quinn.

"Do you have time?" I asked, thinking about his father waiting for him.

It was like he could read my mind. "Trust me — Hunter will track me down eventually. He always does. Besides, he probably just wants to get on my case about the usual."

"What's the usual?" I asked as we left the boards planted in the sand near his house and headed in the direction of my grandparents'.

"School, SATs, college applications — the standard senior-year thing. Basically, my whole future. Fascinating, right?"

"I guess it depends on your future," I said, trying to match his easy tone.

"That's nothing to worry about. Hunter — my dad — has conveniently figured it all out for me."

"Is it? Convenient, I mean."

"It would be if he didn't expect me to follow in his footsteps," said Quinn. "If you're going to be a financial genius, you need to be good with numbers. Places like Wharton and Harvard Business School expect that sort of thing."

"And let me guess," I said. "You're not good with numbers?"

"'Not good' would be the understatement of all time."

We'd arrived at the spot where I'd left my dad's shirt, and I picked it up off the sand. "I don't know if this will make you feel any better, but my mother has this grand plan that I'll take over her company one day. But it's a tech business, and I can barely even figure out how to turn my laptop on and off."

"Mac or PC?" he asked, so seriously that it took me a second to realize he was joking.

I laughed, but I didn't get a chance to answer him before a twiggy, spandex-clad figure sprinted up toward us. It was Patience, dressed in fancy workout clothes, complete with wrap-around shades and a complicated-looking runner's watch. She glanced at Quinn with approval.

"I'm so glad you're making friends, Delia," she said, pumping her arms to keep her heart rate up while she jogged in place. "Gwyneth and I are going to capoeira later. Do you want to join us?"

"Uh —"

"Capoeira builds muscle tone and is an excellent form of self-defense. And some very important people take this class. We won't be leaving for another" — she checked her watch — "forty-seven minutes if you're interested. Quinn, do give my regards to Fiona and tell your father I'll look forward to seeing him again soon."

Then she dashed off.

"She's energetic," said Quinn.

"That's one word for it," I said as I started putting on my cover-up. But I'd forgotten that I'd put my phone in the breast pocket, and it fell out onto the sand as I pulled the shirt over my head. Quinn picked it up and handed it to me.

"Thanks," I said, brushing off the screen. With a jolt, I saw that I'd missed a call. And the caller ID read "Out of Area."

Quinn was saying something, but I didn't really hear him. "Sorry — I, I just need to check this."

"No problem," he said as I punched in my password. The automated voice told me that I had one new message, from an unknown number, sent at 8:32 A.M., and with a duration of fifty-six seconds.

There was a weird rushing noise in my ears, and Quinn and the beach and the ocean seemed to fade away as I waited for the message to play. It felt like the pause lasted forever before a woman's voice finally began to speak.

But it was the wrong woman.

> *Delia, honey, it's Nora. I'm in San Diego, staying at my son's to help with his new baby, and the little devil keeps getting me up at the most ungodly hours. But since I'm up, I figured I'd take advantage of the time difference and see how*

you're settling in with your aunt. Give me a call when you
get a chance, okay, hon?

Then she left her son's number in California, which I didn't
have stored in my address book and which must have been
unlisted to boot. Which was why it had shown up as "Out
of Area."

The disappointment was so intense that it felt like I'd been
punched in the stomach. And this time there was no way to
stop the prickling in my eyes. The tears were already poised
to spill out.

"What is it?" Quinn was asking. "Delia?"

But I didn't trust myself to speak without completely losing
it. All I could do was flee.

Fourteen

I ran blindly toward my grandparents' house, desperate to be where nobody could see me cry. I drew the line at sobbing in front of near-strangers, especially if they looked like Quinn. I heard him calling out, and I almost crashed into Charley on the stairs leading up from the beach, but I mumbled an excuse and pushed past her. I didn't stop running until I'd reached the sanctuary of my mother's old room and the door was safely closed behind me.

As crying fits go, this one was pretty severe. I kept telling myself that nothing had changed — I still knew about the satellite photos, and the first "Out of Area" call was still mysterious. And I tried to reassure myself that I was still going to be able to figure it all out. It was just the collision of a perfect golden morning with a crushing disappointment that had sent me into emotional overload.

By the time Charley knocked on my door, maybe half an hour or so later, the tears had slowed to a trickle, and I had that wrung-out, dazed feeling you get after a session of torrential sobbing. I blew my nose and wiped my eyes and went to open the door.

"Do you want to talk about it?" she asked.

I knew that if I did, the crying would start up all over again, so I shook my head. And being Charley, she didn't press or pry. She only said, "It's probably healthy to let it all out." Then she made a face. "I can't believe I said something that lame. More importantly, have you checked the weather?"

Outside, a mass of purple-black storm clouds had gathered on the horizon. They looked as gloomy as I felt, but Charley had a different take.

"Isn't it fabulous?" she said. "Just the excuse we need to cut out early from the Truesdale house of horrors. And I know the perfect way to spend a rainy day."

I was worried that Charley's idea of a rainy-day good time would involve another shopping trip, and I didn't think I could deal with that many mirrors given what I must look like after all the sobbing. But instead we packed up and went to an enormous multiplex somewhere in the Long Island suburbs.

We watched two movies, played every single arcade game in the lobby, and systematically worked our way through the menu at the concession stand. Then we topped it off with the drive-through window at a Dairy Queen on the way back to the city.

T.K. would've been appalled, and I did feel sort of queasy when it was all over, but Charley was right — it really was the perfect way to spend a rainy day. I even felt recovered enough to tell Charley all about Quinn on the beach, and how different he was from the Quinn at school, and how we'd surfed and I hadn't choked up or embarrassed myself. At least, not until I'd fled.

It was after midnight by the time we got to the loft, and when the elevator doors opened, we walked smack into a tower of cardboard. It turned out that all of my boxes had arrived from Palo Alto, and the super had brought them up and stacked them in the foyer while we were away.

I was too tired to begin unpacking that night, but I got on it as soon as I woke up Sunday morning. I didn't care much about the clothes, though I pretended to for Charley's sake — she was always interested in clothes, even boring, T.K.-approved outfits. But between what she'd bought me and having to wear a uniform most days, I already had everything I'd need for New York. In fact, it would probably be more efficient to leave the boxes packed for my return to Palo Alto, but I couldn't tell Charley that.

Fortunately, she had plans to go to an art show with friends in the afternoon, and when she urged me to come with her, I pled homework. But as soon as she left, I turned my attention to what I was really interested in: the laptop and the file folders I'd grabbed from T.K.'s desk at home.

I didn't know what they'd tell me, if anything — I'd only shoved them in with some sweaters at the last minute, after it became clear that I was being sent to New York no matter how much of a fuss I made — but I was still glad I had them now.

My mother loves her shredder almost as much as her label maker, so I started with the folders. I figured that whatever papers she'd bothered to hold on to had to be important, and that they'd be current, too, since she hadn't yet put them away in her file cabinet. And I also knew they'd be about me, because they were all stowed in the desk drawer marked CORDELIA.

But most of the folders were pretty dull, though they did make me wonder if T.K. was suffering from a kind of obsessive-compulsive disorder that involved giving every single item its own properly labeled home. She'd labeled one folder CORDELIA — FALL CLASS SCHEDULE, and all she'd put in it was a lonely copy of my fall class schedule for West Palo Alto High. Then she'd done the same thing with the schedules for my soccer games and school holidays.

There were only a couple of folders that looked like they might be interesting. The first was labeled CORDELIA — POSSIBILITIES FOR BAYEE, which sounded nice and cryptic. Inside I found a bunch of notes in my mother's writing, scrawled on random scraps of paper and held together with a binder clip.

Deciphering anything T.K.'s written usually takes a while. Part of the reason she loves her label maker so much is that her actual handwriting looks like it belongs to an adolescent boy, so if she wants things to look neat she needs mechanical help. But these notes turned out to be ideas for projects I could do for the Bay Area Young Einstein Expo.

The other folder I thought might be interesting didn't have my name on it, and I thought maybe it had ended up in the Cordelia drawer by accident. It was labeled simply ROSS. I didn't know any Ross except for Ross's Cove, and I'd never heard T.K. mention anyone by that name, so this was even more cryptic, but I'd just learned the hard way not to expect too much from cryptic labels. Inside I found three pieces of paper: a letter, a Post-it, and a drawing.

The letter was on formal stationery, with a logo at the top. It spelled out EAROFO in big capital letters, and below the logo was an address on K Street in Washington, D.C. The letter itself was short but not exactly sweet.

> *Dear Ms. Truesdale,*
>
> *Thank you for your inquiry. Due to the high level of demand for our services, we are unable to accommodate your request.*
>
> *Sincerely,*
> *Melvin P. Stern*
> *Executive Director*

Melvin P. Stern hadn't bothered to personally sign the letter, which seemed sort of rude. Nor was there any indication as to what kind of services he and EAROFO offered that were in such demand.

I Googled EAROFO, but all I learned was that it was a

Greek word for "putrid, rotten, and bad." I doubted that had been what Melvin P. Stern was going for when he named his organization or business or whatever it was — it was more likely to be an acronym for something else. But that something else didn't show up in the search results, and when I looked for an EAROFO Web site, trying all of the standard suffixes — .com, .net, .org, .edu — the browser only returned error messages.

And just in case the letter wasn't insufficiently enlightening on its own, stuck to its bottom was the Post-it. And on the Post-it T.K. had scrawled five words:

Typical! Don't go through Thad.

Which was totally bizarre. As a general rule, Thad knew more about T.K. than T.K. did — I couldn't even begin to imagine what she wouldn't want him to know or why she wouldn't want him to know it. After all, he probably already did know, whether she wanted him to or not.

I flipped to the drawing, but if I was hoping it would explain anything, I was out of luck. It looked like a bad copy of a bad copy of a picture of a bunch of wavy lines in a box. There was no regular pattern to the lines or the stripes they created, though they reminded me of one of those executive toys my dentist had in his waiting room, a Lucite rectangle with layers of different colored sand trapped inside. When you tilted the rectangle, the sand would pour from one end to the other, rearranging itself in new layers. It was better than back issues of *Highlights* and *Family*

Circle, and also pamphlets on the glories of flossing, but that was about it.

Anyhow, this drawing looked like a black-and-white version of that toy. And there wasn't a title or a signature or anything to indicate what it was supposed to be — just some typed numbers and letters in the top right-hand corner of the page:

$$81°S/175°V$$

The numbers and the degree symbols were clear enough, but the letters didn't work on any scale I knew. I mean, for temperatures *F* was Fahrenheit and *C* was Celsius and *K* was Kelvin, but none of those letters were the ones on the page. The *S* could mean South, but that didn't explain what the *V* stood for. And when I typed 81°S/175°V into the search engine, even the Internet was stumped.

I was now officially lost. I had no idea what the stuff in the Ross folder was supposed to mean, or if I should even care about any of it. And there weren't any more folders to go through. So I booted up T.K.'s laptop, thinking that maybe I'd find the source file for the drawing or mentions of Melvin P. Stern or EAROFO on her hard drive that would clue me in.

The laptop was password-protected, and you'd think that someone like T.K., who ran a technology company, would know better than to choose something so easily guessed, but all I had to do was type C-o-r-d-e-l-i-a to log in. And that's when things got seriously strange:

The entire hard drive had been wiped clean.

There were no e-mails — not even in the Sent or Deleted or Junk Mail folders. There were no appointments on her Outlook calendar or Tasks on her To Do list. There were no memos or spreadsheets or PowerPoint slides. There weren't even any photos or music or videos in her media files.

Only the applications were left. Everything else was gone, like she'd never used the computer at all, like it wasn't even hers. But I knew it was hers because I'd seen her using it hundreds of times. And who else would've chosen my name as a password?

The only trace of T.K. I could find was when I tried the Web browser. All of the bookmarks had been erased, too, but when I clicked on the History menu, a list of the sites she'd visited most recently appeared. Of course, every single link led me to information about something called the Protocol on Environmental Protection to the Antarctic Treaty, so this wasn't exactly helpful. I already knew that T.K. was all about environmental protection, and the fact that she'd been heading to Antarctica wasn't much of a secret, either.

The obvious question was, who had gone to all the trouble to erase the files? And the answer there was nearly as obvious. Nora wouldn't have done it, and I definitely didn't do it. And the only other person who'd been in the house before I left was Thad.

But just because I knew who'd done it didn't mean I

understood *why* he'd done it. And knowing that he'd done it was enough to demolish what little trust I'd had in him in the first place.

I was wondering what happens to a laptop if you drop it from a fifth-floor window when Natalie called. And I really hoped she had some encouraging news, because between the Ross file and the empty hard drive, not to mention a junk-food hangover from my excursion with Charley the previous day, I was feeling pretty grim.

"Hi," I said. "How are you?"

"Do you know anything about Patagonia?" asked Natalie.

I'd already figured out that she wasn't big on small talk, but this still seemed like a complete non sequitur, and it didn't help that I couldn't read her expression over the phone. "Uh, sure," I said. "I have a bunch of their stuff for surfing. It's supposed to be really eco-friendly."

"Not that Patagonia — I'm talking about the place in South America that they named the brand after. That's where the call originated. In a province called Aisén, which is in the Chilean part of Patagonia."

She was waiting for me to say something, but suddenly all I could think of was the Chilean sea bass we'd had for dinner in Southampton. "Is that good?"

"It's awesome," said Natalie, and now I could hear the triumph in her voice. "Because Aisén? It's practically next door to where your mom's ship disappeared!"

Fifteen

Of course, by next door, Natalie meant about 2,500 miles from where the *Polar Star* had sent its SOS, give or take a few hundred miles. And this was almost the same as the distance between Charley's apartment and our house in California, which I wouldn't describe as next door, either. But as land went, Aisén was one of the closest places to Antarctica that wasn't actually Antarctica.

We didn't get a chance to talk through what it all meant, though, before Charley came home armed with takeout and DVDs. But we hastily arranged an emergency meeting for the next morning. And when we met on the front steps before school started, Natalie was just as excited as I was about her discovery.

As she put it, "The odds against a coincidence of this magnitude are statistically insurmountable. It's not like you know anyone but your mother who's recently been within a twenty-five-hundred-mile radius of that particular spot, and especially not anyone who has your number and would feel compelled to reach you."

Meanwhile, all she had to do was pull up the Wikipedia

entry for Aisén on her iPhone to show me why there'd only been static on the message, and why I hadn't heard from T.K. again.

The place sounded like something from one of T.K.'s old Outward Bound brochures. It was nearly the size of New York State, but with only a tiny fraction of the population, and it was almost entirely covered by mountains and ice fields. If she didn't have to worry about me and her company and the ozone layer and all of the other stuff she liked to worry about, T.K. would probably be having a fabulous time, eating lichen and scaling glaciers. There weren't even roads for the most part, let alone a high-quality telecommunications infrastructure.

"Which means it's too remote for her to get a decent connection," I said.

"And maybe she can't charge her phone, either," said Natalie. "Her battery must be dead by now."

"So all we need to do is figure out exactly where she is in Aisén and get her out of there," I said, my mind racing ahead.

"Except that's not going to be easy," said Natalie. "You can't just call up the Chilean authorities and expect them to launch a massive search effort."

She had a good point. What was convincing evidence to a couple of high-school students in Manhattan would probably seem less convincing to the Aisén police department, assuming there was such a thing. It wasn't like the least-populous region in Chile was exactly in the running for the next *CSI* franchise.

The bell rang, and the various other students lingering on the steps began heading inside. We joined them, agreeing to continue the discussion when we met up again in physics. "I'm sure we'll think of something," Natalie assured me.

But before first period was even over, I'd already decided for myself what I needed to do. The next step was perfectly clear.

And in a city like New York, with more than eight million people to choose from, how hard could it be to find a private detective with the skills and contacts to get things done in Chile?

■ ■ ■

I was so eager to get online and start researching private detectives that I was tempted to cut out of school early. But Prescott was big on taking attendance, and for all I knew, Patience had some sort of alarm system rigged up to alert her the moment I left campus.

And, if I was being completely honest, the truth was that I didn't want to miss drama. Mr. Dudley was back, and the class was meeting for the first time that afternoon. And while it might not help with the SATs, T.K. herself always says that you shouldn't draw conclusions without a "robust and rigorously tested fact base."

So I suffered through the endless day, even though it felt like somebody had spiked the coffee in the faculty lounge with sedatives. The teachers all seemed to be moving in slow motion, like they knew I was in a hurry and were trying to torment me. But finally last period arrived.

The kids who gathered on the stage in the auditorium were an even mix of juniors and seniors. I was sort of surprised to see Gwyneth there, given that I'd always thought drama required at least some degree of facial movement. But as soon as the teacher walked in, it made more sense. So did the fact that girls outnumbered boys in the class at least two to one.

Mr. Dudley was probably close to thirty, but he was still so ridiculously good-looking that it was jarring to see him there, with us, rather than up on a movie screen or in the pages of a magazine. It was also pretty obvious that Gwyneth wasn't the only one who was more interested in the teacher than what he taught.

But he didn't seem to notice that he was being worshiped. "Let's get started, people," he said, clapping his hands to call the class to order. He had everyone sit in a semicircle on the stage, and then he welcomed us to "the magical world of theater," which he described as "a noble offering, a gift that brings transparency to opacity, bridges cognitive dissonance, and creates community via communication."

I wasn't convinced that even he understood what all of that was supposed to mean, and he spoke with a phony-sounding British accent as he paced back and forth before us. With every word, I grew more convinced that his accent was fake, but Gwyneth didn't seem to mind. She almost had an expression.

After he'd finished his introduction and launched us on a series of breathing exercises, something caught his attention offstage. "No need to be shy," he called. "Come join us in channeling the muse." Seriously. That's what he said.

I was wondering what Dieter would think of Mr. Dudley when Quinn slid into the spot right between Gwyneth and me. We were supposed to have our eyes closed, but even if I hadn't peeked, the way every other sense suddenly snapped into high alert would've told me exactly who it was.

This was the first I'd seen of him since Saturday, though I had to admit to doing some reliving of that morning over and over again in my head. And we were all supposed to be concentrating on exhaling from our solar plexus, assuming we knew where that was, so it wasn't exactly a good time to turn to Quinn and explain why I'd fled from him on the beach. But it felt incredibly awkward sitting next to him, not saying anything to each other and with the memory of my impromptu exit sort of hanging there in the air.

Little did I know just how much more awkward things were about to get.

We finished the breathing exercises, and Mr. Dudley began detailing his plans for the semester. "Next week, each of you will be performing before the class in scenes I've culled from some of the most important works in the theatrical canon. Please note that this performance will count for a significant percent of your final grade. And people, be warned that I demand the highest standards of professionalism — there will be no tolerance for the dilettantish or the jejune."

"Did he really just say jejune?" Quinn said in a low voice.

Mr. Dudley had been facing away from us, but his hearing must have been incredibly sharp. He whipped his head around and fixed Quinn with a glare that he probably thought was piercing. He consulted a list of students on a clipboard. "Mr. Riley, correct?"

"Yes, sir. Quinn Riley."

"And you are?" Now he was looking at me.

"Delia Truesdale," I answered.

He ran his finger down his list. "Ah, yes. Here you are. Cordelia Truesdale. Someone in your family must be a *King Lear* fan."

"Uh-huh," I said. Besides the extreme sports, Ash had been totally into Shakespeare, but I wasn't going to explain about Ash to Mr. Dudley.

He struck a pose. "'How sharper than a serpent's tooth it is to have a thankless child!'" Then he sighed. "But she wasn't thankless, was she? Poor misunderstood Cordelia."

"Uh-huh," I said again. Mostly I was trying not to cringe.

"Well, Cordelia, since you and Mr. Riley are apparently keen to start rehearsing lines, you can be the first to perform for the class. Next" — he checked his calendar — "Monday. That gives you a full week to prepare." Then he consulted another list on his clipboard. "Hmm. Now which one shall it be? The Bard, perhaps? It only seems fitting."

Given the nonstop randomness that seemed to be the rest of my life, I probably should've expected what would happen next.

"Ah," he said, tapping his finger against one of the items on his list. "This will be perfect for you, Cordelia. Not *Lear* — too challenging for the novice thespian, of course. But Juliet. And you, Mr. Riley — you'll be her Romeo."

Sixteen

I had to give Mr. Dudley credit for choosing something more original than the balcony scene or the death scene or anything that obvious. But he did manage to select a scene with so much potential for embarrassment that it might as well have been a death scene.

Act I, scene 5, to be specific. And in case you're a bit rusty on your *Romeo and Juliet,* here's an excerpt:

ROMEO
Thus from my lips, by yours, my sin is purged.

JULIET
Then have my lips the sin that they have took.

ROMEO
Sin from thy lips? O trespass sweetly urged!
Give me my sin again.

JULIET
You kiss by the book.

Yes, that's right. There was kissing.

To be clear, it wasn't like I wasn't interested in kissing Quinn.

But I hadn't expected it to happen in front of an audience.

The fact was, I hadn't expected it to happen at all, since the last he'd seen of me was my back as I sprinted away from him. I was starting to miss those days when he still only thought I was a brain-dead mute and hadn't realized I was also an emotional basket case.

Mr. Dudley took up so much time assigning scenes and parts and urging us to channel the muse again and saying a lot of other inane things that class ended before any rehearsing could take place.

Which was just as well, because if I was worried about Quinn thinking I had a split personality, what little interaction we ended up having after the bell rang left me more worried about *his* split personality.

The Quinn from the beach, the guy who woke up at dawn to teach Bea and Oliver to surf and who told me about his father and math and his future — that Quinn was nowhere in sight. But Apathy Quinn was back in a major way.

I was all ready to apologize and explain everything, but here's the conversation we had instead:

DELIA

Uh, hi.

QUINN
Hey.

DELIA
So, um —

OFFSTAGE MINION
Master Q. You coming with?

QUINN
Juliet, huh?

DELIA
Guess so. Listen, I sort of owe you an ap —

OFFSTAGE MINION
Riley? Where are you?

QUINN
[To offstage minion]
Be right there.
[To delia]
Later, Juliet.

EXIT QUINN

And then he was gone, just like in the stairwell and the cafeteria. And definitely not like on the beach.

I knew I shouldn't dwell. After all, I had more urgent things to worry about, like rescuing my mother from the Chilean wilderness.

But not dwelling would have been a whole lot easier if Apathy Quinn and Beach Quinn didn't have the same gray-green eyes.

■　■　■

Charley wasn't home when I got back to the loft after school, but that suited my plans perfectly. I booted up my laptop and started Googling private detectives.

It turned out that I might have been a bit too confident about how simple it would be to find what I was looking for. I mean, I never would've guessed that there were so many licensed professionals who'd like to help me check up on a cheating spouse or fraudulent insurance claims. And if I required armed guards, nanny checks, or litigation support, the world was my oyster.

But strangely, none of the listings I found said anything like: "Accomplished Spanish-Speaking Private Investigator with Expertise in Remote South American Missing Persons Search Available for Immediate Hire."

And even if I ever did find the sort of person I needed, it looked like I might also have been a bit too confident about being able to pay him. Based on the rates I'd seen posted on some of the Web sites, it would definitely cost more money than I could access on my own. A lot more money.

I did have an allowance from the trust T.K. had set up. It covered basic needs like my phone bill and ice cream and the occasional minor shopping spree, but that was about as far as it went. Even if I cut out all nonessentials, it wouldn't be anywhere near enough.

In theory, I was supposed to go to Patience if I wanted to tap into the additional funds from my mother. But asking Patience for cash for this specific purpose would be like getting down on my knees and begging her to commit me to the nearest psychiatric ward. And just about everyone else I knew would have as much of a problem as I did coming up with that much ready cash.

My only real option was Charley. I was worried about asking her — I'd been so careful to avoid the topic of my mother altogether since I'd overheard her talking to Patience — but I also didn't have much of a choice. At least, not if I wanted to keep moving things forward.

The information about the call originating in Chile had made everything seem so obvious and right when I was talking it through with Natalie. I just hoped it would be enough to keep Charley from thinking I'd completely lost it when I explained what I needed and why.

■　　■　　■

By the time Charley got home, it was nearly eight. She'd spent the entire day at the post-production facility where they were editing the film, and she was, typically, starving. "I'm thinking spring rolls and pad thai and the lemongrass chicken thing and also maybe some of that beef with the ginger. And you can drink all of the soda you want, and I get to have an enormous martini to erase the ridiculous day I just had."

Charley's favorite Thai restaurant was only a few blocks away. I figured it couldn't hurt to wait until she had some martini in her before I told her that I still thought T.K. was alive and needed money for a detective, so I sat patiently until she had the drink in hand, complete with the six olives she'd requested. (Charley prefers her vegetables in the form of garnish.)

But before she'd taken even a single sip, something incredibly strange happened.

"I was speaking to Patty, and there's something I need to run by you," she said.

That wasn't the strange part, though the words "I was speaking to Patty" weren't exactly a promising start.

"We were discussing how reaching closure can't be easy when there's so much uncertainty about what happened to your mom. So there's someone I'd like you to see."

"Oh?" I said, instantly alarmed. Charley had rolled her eyes when she said it, but the use of a word like "closure" still implied that my aunts had been in touch with a psychiatrist or grief counselor or someone like that. But I couldn't believe that Charley would sell me out that way, especially not after the agreement we'd made. And this sort of setup was going to make the conversation I actually wanted to have with her that much more difficult.

Charley took a look at my face and laughed. It must've been pretty obvious what was going through my head. "It's not what you think," she said. "You know I wouldn't do that to you."

"Then what is it?"

"I've found a woman who specializes in situations with a lot of unanswered questions. Her name is Carolina Cardenas, and she's supposed to be the best at this sort of thing. She just moved to New York last year from Ecuador, of all places, but she's already solved a robbery and a kidnapping. The police use her, and she even consults for the FBI. And you have an appointment with her tomorrow afternoon."

I was completely floored. It was like Charley really could read my mind.

Her motivations might be different — she was probably thinking that Carolina Cardenas would prove that T.K. was dead, not that she'd help me locate her and get her home — but the critical thing was that she'd gone out and found me a detective without my even having to ask.

And not just any detective, but a native Spanish speaker with South American connections, which was exactly what I needed.

The only way it could've been better was if this Cardenas person had been from Chile, but Ecuador was pretty close. I mean, they were on the same continent and everything.

If I hadn't been wedged behind a table stacked with dishes of food, I would've jumped up to hug Charley. "That's perfect," I said. "Absolutely perfect."

"You'll have to skip your last class, but I'm guessing you won't mind," she said.

"No, that's okay. It's drama, but we meet every day, so it's not a big deal."

"Drama? Are you sure? Why don't I reschedule it for when you can miss something better? What time is physics? Or what about gym? When's gym?"

"No, really, it's fine." I didn't want to run the risk of having to wait longer for an appointment, and it wasn't like Quinn had been sweeping me off my feet or anything. "But speaking of drama," I said, "guess who's been cast as the Romeo to my Juliet."

"You're playing Juliet? That's fabulous! When did this happen? Do I get to see it? Dieter's convinced you have Ze Presence with a capital Z and a capital P — he keeps pestering me about putting you in his next film. When do you open? Can I help you rehearse?"

"It's only part of one scene, not the whole play, and it's just for the class, not a real performance. And Quinn Riley. That's who's playing Romeo."

She gave a little shriek, and people in the restaurant turned to stare. "No!"

"Yes," I confirmed.

"That's fabulous! It's fate! But why are you so calm? And how did you wait until now to tell me something this monumental?"

"Don't get too excited. Apathy Quinn is back." And I told her about what happened after class.

"You know, I've been thinking about Apathy Quinn and Beach Quinn. It's like sometimes he's the Andrew McCarthy character from *Pretty in Pink*, and then other times he's like the James Spader character. The question is which one is the real Quinn. But at least he's not Ducky, thank God, because he was annoying."

"You're losing me," I said.

"Don't tell me you haven't seen *Pretty in Pink*." She was astounded.

"I've heard of it, I just haven't seen it."

"Don't joke about something this serious."

"I'm not joking."

She pointed a chopstick at me. "Just because a movie's older than you, it's no excuse for such a gaping hole in your cultural literacy."

"But —"

"This calls for emergency measures. We'll get this packed up and finish eating at home," she said, scanning the room for our waitress. "There's not a second to waste."

Seventeen

Charley and I stayed up way too late watching *Pretty in Pink* and eating Thai food, but I still woke up the next morning before my alarm went off, like my subconscious wanted to tell me something.

I'd been having a dream about surfing with Quinn, and while you didn't have to be Freud to come up with theories about that, I still felt like I was somehow missing the point. It wasn't until I'd spent a full five minutes lying in bed, sleepily contemplating the wedge of light between the windowsill and the bottom of the shade, that I figured out what the point was.

I leaped up and dashed to my computer. I'd never heard back from any of the bloggers I contacted about the satellite photos, but I'd bookmarked their blogs. Now I pulled up the first one and scrolled down through the more recent posts to find the right images.

There were a lot of posts, on a lot of different topics, but I couldn't find the one I wanted, so I decided it must be in the archives. There I found hundreds of old posts, going back several years, but none of them was the one about the *Polar Star's* disappearance. Which was strange.

I searched the second blog. And then I searched the third blog. A prickling feeling ran along my spine as I clicked from page to page.

All of the posts about the satellite photos were gone.

Maybe if one of the bloggers had taken down his post, I'd understand. Even if two had done it, I might be able to come up with some sort of explanation.

But all three?

■　■　■

Natalie responded to my text within seconds, and we met in what was becoming our usual spot on the steps in front of school. I handed her my laptop and watched as her fingers attacked the keyboard.

"I'm checking your cache files," she explained. "Sometimes your browser will store copies of pages from the Web sites you visit, so that it doesn't have to ping the site's server again if you go back — it just returns the page you were looking at before. What were the URLs for the blogs again?"

The next thing I knew, she'd pulled up a copy of the blog post that was no longer on the blog itself. "You made it look so easy," I marveled.

"It was," she said. "Now what did you want to show me?"

"Here," I said, pointing to the screen. "See the time stamp on the photo with the *Polar Star*? And then the time stamp on the other one, where the ship has disappeared, is for a few minutes later, right?"

"Uh-huh," she said.

"But the angle of the sun is a lot steeper in the second photograph — you can tell by the way the light looks on the water and the shadows on the whitecaps. Does the sun move a lot faster in Antarctica than it does here?"

"It's not the sun moving, it's the earth moving," Natalie said automatically, but she'd already pulled out a small ruler from her bag and was holding it against the images on the screen, measuring the shadows cast by the waves. Then she took out a calculator and began jotting down numbers on a piece of graph paper. I didn't even try to follow whatever it was she was doing.

She filled the sheet with equations and calculations, peering from the screen to her calculator and then back to the graph paper again. It was almost time for class to start before she drew a line under a final number and put her pencil down.

"There," she said with satisfaction. "This will be somewhat imprecise without knowing the exact orbital position of the earth on the date in question — I can look that up later if you want — but my calculations are directionally correct. And they indicate that the second picture was actually taken at least two hours *before* the picture with the earlier time stamp. Somebody must have swapped out the real picture with the older one and then added the fake time stamp."

I was in awe. "You're good," I said.

"This is pretty basic stuff," she said modestly.

I thought about the two-hour gap, and the disconnect with the time stamps, and what it all meant. "So the *Polar Star* could have sent out the SOS and then just gone radio silent and sailed away before anyone got there."

"There was more than enough time," said Natalie.

"But why?" I asked. "And then who switched the photos and changed the time stamps?"

"It had to be someone with access to the site that posted the original images, which probably means they control the satellite, too," said Natalie. "And that rules out a lot of people. It's not like you can go buy a satellite at the drugstore and launch it from your backyard. They cost millions of dollars. I think they're regulated, too. A government or a big corporation is probably involved."

"So we're up against a government or a corporation?" I asked.

"Or someone with the power to manipulate a government or a corporation," said Natalie. "Oh, and don't forget the power to convince all the bloggers to take down their posts and not respond to your e-mails."

She said this like it was no big deal, but I suddenly felt very small.

■   ■   ■

After a morning and lunch period without any Quinn sightings, I got a text from Charley. She was stuck in the editing room with Dieter and Helga, but she'd join me for my appointment as soon as she could get away.

That was okay with me — if anything, I'd probably be more comfortable without Charley there. That way I could explain about all of the things I'd found out on my own without having to feel guilty when she realized just how much I'd been hiding from her.

I'd sort of been picturing Carolina Cardenas in a run-down office, with her name stenciled on the door in peeling paint. She'd be wearing a fedora and chain-smoking, and every so often she'd take a bottle out of her desk drawer and pour a shot of whisky into a coffee mug. Of course, I'd also been picturing everything in black and white, since the phrase "private detective" made me think of an old Humphrey Bogart movie I'd once watched with Nora.

Instead, Charley's directions took me to a neighborhood on the Lower East Side that was a mix of restaurants and shops and tenements in varying stages of gentrification. The signs hanging in the windows were in just about every language you could imagine, and twenty-somethings with lots of tattoos and piercings shared the sidewalks with yuppies and Hasidic Jews and Chinese. I felt a bit out of place in my plaid kilt and blazer, but nobody paid much attention to me.

The address I was looking for was on Essex Street, in one of the tenement buildings that wasn't being renovated. It was so different from what I'd expected that I almost called Charley to make sure I had it right. But C. CARDENAS was clearly written on a label next to the buzzer marked 3F.

Of course, the fact that it was written in purple sparkle pen should have clued me in immediately, but I was getting used to Charley finding the most unconventional way to accomplish even the most conventional goals.

The outside door clicked open before I could ring, so I assumed that the detective had some way of knowing I'd arrived. The same thing happened when I reached the third floor — the Europop that was blasting from behind 3F stopped abruptly, and the door swung open before I could raise my fist to knock.

Going by Carolina Cardenas's receptionist, this time Charley just might have outdone herself on the unconventional front. The girl at the door was maybe a few years older than me, but even smaller, with wavy brown hair hanging almost to her waist. She wore a tiny miniskirt and a tinier halter top, and each of the toenails on her bare feet was painted a different color.

"You are Delia, *sí?*" she asked with a friendly smile.

"*Sí.* I mean, yes."

"It is a delight to know you. Your auntie, she is still with the scarf man, *sí?* No worries, we do not have the need to wait for her. Please, come in, okay?"

"Okay. Thank you." I followed her into a room that was furnished in a combination of Ikea and flea market.

"Please, you seat yourself here, okay?" She indicated one of a mismatched pair of canvas director's chairs at a bright yellow plastic table, and I obediently sat myself. "Can I offer you a beverage refreshment? I have the Coca-Cola Light and the Strawberry Quik, also. You like the Strawberry Quik?"

"Oh, no, that's all right. Thank you, though."

"Then we will commence, okay?"

"Okay."

I was thinking that meant that she would go get Carolina Cardenas or take me to another room that was more of an office. Not that there seemed to be any other rooms. Instead she sat down at the table across from me and grabbed my hand.

"Ay!" she said, as if I'd given her an electric shock. "You are very noisy."

"Excuse me?" I said, trying, unsuccessfully, to get my hand back.

"You have many things in your head that are making the noise. *Sí?*" Her big brown eyes stared into mine, and her free hand played with a crystal charm that dangled from a ribbon around her neck.

And that's when I realized why Charley announcing that she was sending me to a private detective had seemed so strange.

She hadn't been sending me to a private detective.

This girl wasn't Carolina Cardenas's secretary or receptionist. She was Carolina Cardenas. And Carolina Cardenas wasn't a detective.

She was a psychic. A psychic being much less of a strange idea coming from Charley than a private detective.

I probably wasn't doing a very good job of hiding what I was thinking. "You have the big surprise," Carolina said with a giggle. "You are expecting that I am the *investigadora*, like in the *Angels of Charlie, sí*?"

"Uh —"

"Do not worry yourself," she said. "I can still help, even if I am not the *investigadora*. Your auntie, she says you are having the questions. I am seeing that. So many questions!" Her brow furrowed. "But not the questions she says."

Given my parents and everything they were all about, I probably should have been trying to figure out how I could make a graceful exit. I mean, psychics are pretty much the opposite of scientific method. But I'd watched enough *Medium* on TV to be curious about what Carolina could tell me. I'd just have to make sure that T.K. never found out about this. Or Erin. Or Justin. Or even Natalie. I didn't think I could handle the mocking.

"I know, you are having the doubts," Carolina said. "But I can give you answers. Like, you know, the Ross you are wondering about, the one in the picture? It is a place, not a person. And it is not the place you are already knowing, the place where you do the surfing. This Ross is very cold, with the water and the wind and the ice. And the, how do you say in English, *los pingüinos*, the funny birds in the coats?"

"Penguins?" I said reflexively.

"*Sí, sí*, the penguins."

Now she was totally freaking me out. "How do you know all that?" I asked.

She shrugged. "Some of it, I know from your head. The rest I just know from my own head. It is that way since I was a baby. Now, you want to talk about your mama, *sí*?"

After what she'd said about Ross, I was scared to hear how she'd answer my next question. But I took a deep breath and made myself say the words. "Is she — is she alive?"

"Your mama? It is certain she is alive," Carolina said in surprise, like I'd asked her something so basic she couldn't understand why I'd bothered.

And though I'd been telling myself the same thing, and in spite of knowing about Aisén and everything, listening to her say this with such confidence made me practically giddy with relief. Only when I finally exhaled did I realize I'd been holding my breath. "Then do you know where she is?"

Carolina frowned, concentrating. "I see her, but it is not easy. She worries about you, but she does not want to be seen. And the place she is in, it is very beautiful and wild, but not warm. There are the big mountains, also with the ice, and there is water. But it is not the Ross place. It is a different place. But you should not be worrying yourself. She is safe. And she also is with the *novio*."

"What's a *novio*?" I asked.

"You know, the boyfriend."

"Boyfriend?" As far as I knew, T.K. hadn't gone on a single date since my dad died. "Are you sure about that?"

"Certainly I am sure," said Carolina, like I'd offended her. "Why would I be saying such a thing if it is not true? You will be meeting him when you see your mama."

I forgot about the *novio*. "When will that be?" I asked eagerly.

"Soon," she said. "In eight."

"Eight what?"

"Ay! That is what is not clear. I am thinking and thinking and thinking, since your auntie was calling, but all I see is eight." She screwed her eyes shut, like she was trying extra hard to focus, and gripped my hand more tightly. "Maybe eight weeks? Or months? I do not think years, but it is possible. I am sorry, I wish I could be telling you more exactly. But you will see her in eight."

"Okay," I said, trying to quell the panic set off by the "eight years" comment.

She opened her eyes. "Now, you must not say anything about this to your aunties. They are not ready to know what is true, so it will only make trouble. And then the eight becomes ten or twelve. This is very important. You understand?"

Hearing about ten or twelve didn't help with the panic,

either, but then Carolina abruptly changed course. "Now, let us be talking about you. You are the artist, *sí?*"

"What? Uh, no. I'm in high school."

"But you have the art. You are a performer."

"I'm supposed to be in a play, but —"

"I see the, *cómo se dice,* the kissing, *sí?*" She giggled again. "And the Romeo, he is just like you."

"How is the Romeo just like me?"

"You are both missing your mamas."

According to Charley, Quinn had pretty much sent his mama packing, so I didn't see how he could be missing her. "Why is he missing his ma — I mean, his mother?" I started to ask. But just then Carolina's hand went suddenly cold and clammy and slipped out of my grasp.

She moaned. "*Ay, Dios.*"

"Carolina? Are you all right?"

She'd gone pale beneath the olive of her complexion, and she held her fingers to the sides of her head. "It will be okay," she said, but her teeth were clenched like she was in pain.

I jumped up. "I'll call a doctor."

"No, no doctor. This is just what is happening sometimes, when I do the reading. I get the ache of the head."

"Can I get you some aspirin, then? Or maybe you should lie down?" I reached to help her up.

She cried out at my touch and jerked away.

"What's wrong?" I asked in alarm.

"Red," she said. "It feels all red."

"What feels all red?"

"You do. And that means danger." Her dark eyes were enormous in her ashen face.

"Danger?"

"Yes. Danger. For you."

Eighteen

With that, Carolina staggered over to the sofa and collapsed into a ball on the cushions. A second later, she started to snore, enormous, honking snores that sounded like they couldn't possibly come from such a tiny person.

I waited for a while to make sure there wasn't anything seriously wrong with her, but the color was already returning to her face as she slept, and her hands had lost that cold, clammy feeling. After ten minutes or so, I covered her with a blanket patterned in Hello Kitty characters and quietly let myself out.

I ran into Charley on the sidewalk in front of the building, her finger poised at the buzzer for 3F. "Oh, no," she said, disappointed. "Did I miss the entire thing?"

"We just finished," I said.

"How was it?" she asked.

I was still reeling from Carolina's final warning, but that didn't mean I'd forgotten what she'd said about T.K. not wanting to be found. And with the exception of the *novio*, everything else had been so on target that I wasn't about to disregard her insistence that my "aunties" would only make trouble if they knew. The last thing I needed was anything that would turn the "eight" into a larger number.

So I just said in what I hoped was a convincing way, "She was really helpful. Thank you for setting it up."

I could tell Charley wanted the details, but she was good at knowing when not to push. "We can arrange another appointment for you. I was thinking I might schedule one myself. There are some things I wouldn't mind running by her."

"Like what?" I asked as she flagged down a cab to take us back to the loft.

"Like should I keep my date tonight or stay home and eat leftover Thai food with you? I bet you've never seen *Valley Girl*. It has Nicolas Cage from before he got creepy, and you're in luck, because I own it on both DVD and VHS."

I managed to convince Charley not to cancel, though I think that was mostly because her date was named Bill and he'd grown up in the Midwest. Since the guys she usually went out with came from places you needed a passport to get to, a corn-fed American seemed exotic to her. "I wonder where he'll take me?" she said. "Wouldn't it be fabulous if it's one of those places with checked tablecloths and jalapeño poppers and frozen drinks? And maybe brownie sundaes for dessert?"

It took forever to get her ready, because choosing an outfit was even more of a challenge when there was a chance her date would be wearing Dockers. But I finally got her out the door, noticing as I did that eight P.M. had come and gone uneventfully. Then I took a carton of Thai leftovers from the refrigerator and settled myself at the table with a fork and my laptop.

I had plenty of homework, but I'd already discovered that most of my teachers were willing to cut me some slack since they thought I was recently orphaned. There was also a packet of documents from Thad's secretary, but I pushed it aside. As far as I could tell, they were all about company business, and not about why Thad had erased T.K.'s hard drive or what exactly his role was in this whole mess.

Right now, my highest priority was to find a real detective. For whatever reason, T.K. wanted everyone to think she was dead. And that had to mean that someone or something was a threat to her, and it also had to mean that she couldn't come back until the coast was clear.

I had no idea how she'd ended up in such a situation — she was like the poster child for law-abiding citizens. She even took the speed limit as a literal limit, rather than just a casual suggestion. But one thing was obvious: If T.K. was on the side of right, then whoever was such a threat to her had to be up to no good. They had to be incredibly dangerous, too — otherwise she'd never have felt it necessary to go to such an extreme.

So, I was way out of my league at this point, and Carolina Cardenas telling me I felt all red hadn't exactly been a soothing experience. If I wanted to get to the bottom of things, I was in desperate need of professional help.

I still had the list I'd made the previous day of private investigators. To be on the safe side, I created a new e-mail account using only my first and middle names, and then I e-mailed the investigators that seemed most promising, explaining as discreetly as I could what I was looking for and signing my name as Delia Navare.

And just as I sent off the last e-mail, an IM popped up from Erin.

> WIDGETTE: OMG!
> DELIATRUE: ?
> WIDGETTE: finally!!
> DELIATRUE: J??
> WIDGETTE: asked me 2 geolog symposium at S'ford — plate tectonics!!!
> DELIATRUE: is that good?
> WIDGETTE: subduction + statigraphy = tru romance!!!!

Erin and Justin had been in love with each other since the third grade, not that either of them had ever acted on it, so this was exciting, and we had to IM for a while about what she should wear. I had to force myself to sign off and get back to work if I wanted to follow up on everything Carolina had told me before Charley returned.

For starters, I Googled "Ross" and "penguins." And in case

I'd had any doubts left about Carolina's abilities, this pretty much vanquished them. Smack-dab in the Southern Ocean, practically next to the Amundsen Sea and where it almost definitely would've been the next stop on the *Polar Star's* itinerary, was the Ross Sea. The Ross Sea was adjacent to the Ross Ice Shelf, which looked like penguin heaven as far as I could tell from the photos I found on the Web.

Of course, just because I now knew what the label on the Ross folder referred to didn't mean I understood all of the stuff in it — only that it was relevant. So next I Googled "Melvin Stern."

It turned out that Melvin was a really popular name for Mr. and Mrs. Sterns who wanted their sons to grow up to be doctors. There was a psychiatrist Melvin Stern in Colorado and an oncologist Melvin Stern in Kansas and an orthopedist Melvin Stern in Texas, but I didn't think any of them was the Melvin Stern I wanted.

It wasn't until I tried "Melvin P. Stern" that I struck gold. Because while there was a Dr. Melvin P. Stern practicing proctology in Connecticut, there was also just a plain old Melvin P. Stern in Washington, D.C. And this Melvin P. Stern was the executive director of a political action committee called End American Reliance on Foreign Oil.

So EAROFO was an acronym, just like I'd thought. But the only information I could find about it was in an online directory of political action committees and other types of lobbyists in Washington. The entry didn't give any detail about its activities, but it did provide the names and titles of its board members. And every single one was the CEO or chairman of an oil company. Some of them were both.

The pieces were starting to come together. On a hunch, I typed in "Ross Sea" and "oil." Somehow I wasn't surprised when this led me to a discussion of the Protocol on Environmental Protection to the Antarctic Treaty — the same treaty T.K. had been looking up on the Web. And I was even less surprised when I read that the treaty's key provision was an international ban on oil exploration and drilling in specific areas of the Antarctic, including the Ross Sea.

That's when another IM popped up, this time from Justin.

JUSTROCKS: sup?

DELIATRUE: congrats!

JUSTROCKS: ?

DELIATRUE: E luvs geology

JUSTROCKS: she told u?!

DELIATRUE: plate tectonics = romance. or something like that

JUSTROCKS: ha. anyhow — no big deal

He could pretend to be blasé, but I knew he was psyched. And since I also knew he'd never come right out and ask, I told him what to wear, too. I might not be able to tell Charley about the other things I'd been up to, but I was looking forward to telling her about how my two best friends were going to a lecture about rocks on their first date. She hadn't entirely believed me when I'd tried to explain what Silicon Valley was really like.

And maybe it was all of the thinking about rocks that did it, because as soon as I logged off with Justin, the final puzzle piece snapped into place. I grabbed the mysterious copy of a copy of a drawing from the folder. Suddenly, I knew exactly what it was.

It wasn't some sort of abstract art experiment, or anything nearly that obscure. It was a geologic map. The different layers were actually different strata of the earth's crust, shown in cross-section. Even I could remember that much from ninth-grade earth science.

And when I pulled up a regular map of the Ross Sea on my computer screen, it was right there, staring me in the face: The coordinates for the Ross Sea were 81° South and 175° West. The same numbers as on the drawing, except the *W* for West must have gotten cut off when it had been Xeroxed, which was why it looked like a *V.*

I'd bet anything that somewhere in those layers of earth, beneath the freezing polar waters, was oil. Oil that could go a long way to reducing, if not completely ending, American reliance on foreign oil for a really long time. Of course, to get at it, you'd have to violate the treaty.

And I'd also bet that T.K., obsessive labeler and filer that she was, would never have included all of those items in the same folder by accident.

Which could only mean that the oil company executives of EAROFO, the oil under the Ross Sea, and maybe even Thad, were all inextricably tied together.

Nineteen

I met Natalie before school again, and this time I told her about Carolina and also everything I'd learned about EAROFO and the Ross Sea and the oil. She was eager to study the geologic map for herself, but she was less thrilled about Carolina.

"I don't believe in psychics," she said. "Are you sure your aunt hadn't already told her all about you, so she'd know what to say? Or maybe she researched you on the Internet or something? That's how these people work. They find out something about you, and then they play off your reactions and what you tell them."

"How could she know about Ross?"

"Are you absolutely sure you didn't mention it yourself?"

"I'm positive. And she definitely came up with Romeo on her own, too."

"That could have been a lucky guess. I mean, every girl has a crush on someone — she could have meant it as a generic term." I'd told Natalie about Quinn and drama, but she'd figured out the crush part by herself.

Mostly Natalie seemed offended that Carolina could just

know things, rather than having to study and analyze to get to the answer. It was like an insult to her entire worldview. But she did agree with Carolina about the one thing I thought she'd have dismissed as melodramatic psychic-babble.

"Look," she said. "We know that someone powerful is behind the changes to the satellite photos and that there's big money behind EAROFO. And it sounds like your mother was on to something that nobody wanted her to know. So, if they went after your mother, won't they come after you if you start asking the same questions?"

If she was trying to make me feel better about Carolina's warning, she wasn't doing a very good job. I mean, there's nothing like the most rational person you know on the East Coast agreeing with the most irrational thing a psychic has said to really drive a point home.

The bell went off right then, and my phone began to ring at the exact same time, so Natalie went ahead while I picked up the call. The screen showed a New York area code, and I was hoping it would be one of the detectives I'd contacted.

But it was Patience instead. "Ridiculous," she said. "Absolutely ridiculous."

"Uh, hi?" I said.

"I don't know what that man thinks he's doing, but it's unacceptable. And it's impossible to get him on the phone to explain himself."

She had to rant a bit more before I could figure out which man she was talking about and what was so ridiculous and unacceptable. It turned out that Patience had received her own copies of the documents Thad sent me, and she was a lot more interested than I'd been in what they said. She'd also read beyond the first two lines of the first document, which was as far as I'd gotten.

According to her, the net impact of the proposals in the documents was that Thad would have more responsibility and I would have less. I didn't really want any responsibility, so this would have been fine if I had even the slightest trust left in Thad.

But Patience now trusted him even less than I did. She said Thad was trying to alienate me from my birthright — her word, not mine — which to her was like a declaration of war. And you really, really didn't want to be at war with Patience. If Thad hadn't been such a weasel, I would've felt sorry for him.

"I'll let you know when I'm able to schedule a call with this Wilcox person, but don't worry, Cordelia — we will not be authorizing a single one of these outrageous proposals," she assured me.

She wasn't big on good-byes, either, so I was standing there talking into a dead phone when Quinn brushed past on his way inside.

"Morning, Juliet," he said.

And because I was overwhelmed by EAROFO and Natalie's warning and Patience and everything else, all so early in the morning, the sound of his voice instantly brought on a minor fit of brain paralysis. Not that it mattered, since he was gone almost before I'd realized he was there and meanwhile my phone was ringing again.

I picked it up without checking the screen since I assumed it would be Patience, ranting about whatever she'd forgotten to rant about before.

But this call really was from a detective.

It was hard to catch his name because it was so long and Spanish-sounding. And he wasn't one of the detectives I'd contacted, but a colleague had forwarded him my e-mail. He also had an appointment available that afternoon and would be delighted to see if he could help.

I did some quick thinking. I'd have to skip drama again, but this was much more important. And while today I didn't have a note from Charley to excuse me, I told him I'd be there anyhow.

I had an idea about how I could get out of class without my aunts finding out.

Twenty

I'm an only child, and I'd always lived a relatively crime-free life, so I didn't have that much experience when it came to manipulating friends or relatives. But it was pretty easy to blackmail Gwyneth. I tracked her down at lunch, which for her consisted of pickles, Fritos, and Tab. "Hi," I said.

She gave me a blank stare, but that was her usual expression, so I took it as a positive sign.

"Can you forge your mom's handwriting?" I asked.

At close range and under bright light it might have been possible to detect her head move in a very slight up-and-down direction, so I decided she'd nodded.

"Then could you write a note getting me out of last period and give it to Mr. Dudley?"

Gwyneth slowly took a bite of pickle and just as slowly chewed and swallowed. "She can't do it herself?"

I gave her my most meaningful look. "There are some things she's better off not knowing."

My most meaningful look met with another blank stare.

"Don't you agree?" I asked with a pointed nod in the direction of a water glass on the table nearby. "About how there are some things your mother's better off not knowing?"

It was possible she didn't even realize I was blackmailing her, because her expression didn't change, or maybe it did but so slightly I couldn't tell. Either way, she unzipped her Prada bag and pulled out some stationery with *Patience Truesdale Babbitt* engraved on it in a swirling font. "I'll get Grey to do it," she said. "He's better at her signature."

■　■　■

The detective's name was Rafael Francisco Valenzuela Sáenz de Santamaría, and while his office didn't look like Humphrey Bogart's, it still looked a lot more like an office than Carolina Cardenas's studio apartment. It was on the fourth floor of an actual office building, and his name was on the door and everything. He also had framed certificates on the wall that declared him to be a licensed private investigator, and he was wearing a suit and tie. So even though the tie had dancing ponies on it, I felt like things were off to a good start.

He settled me in a chair and then sat down behind his desk to face me. He was probably in his thirties, with dark brown hair and warm brown eyes behind little round glasses. And if he was surprised by my age or Prescott uniform, he didn't show it. He just clasped his hands in front of him, smiled in a friendly way, and said, "How can I be of assistance, Miss Navare?"

"Well, Mr. —" I realized I had no idea where his last name began in the string of names on the door.

He chuckled. "Call me Rafe. Everyone does, even my family back in Colombia."

"Okay. Then you'll have to call me Delia."

Once we'd agreed on what to call each other, and once he'd assured me that our conversation would be completely confidential, I told him the whole story. I started at the very beginning, when T.K. left for her trip, and I finished with my theories about why she'd want people to think she was dead.

He listened carefully, taking notes and asking the occasional question. When I'd finished, he took off his glasses and rubbed at the red mark they left on the bridge of his nose. Then he leaned back in his chair and looked up at the ceiling, like he was thinking. And after he thought for a bit, he sat up straight again and put his glasses back on. "Interesting," he said. "Very interesting."

"Do you think you can help?" I asked.

"I don't want to make any promises, Delia. But let me poke around and see what I can find out."

I was so relieved that he hadn't been skeptical or dismissive, and so happy to hear him say he'd poke around, that I almost forgot about my little problem.

"Um, about your fee —" I said.

He brushed the question aside. "Let's not worry about that right now. If I decide to take the case, we can discuss it then."

I refused to get caught up on the "if I decide" part. I was sure that once he saw how much substance there was to everything I'd told him, he'd definitely have to take the case. "That sounds great," I said.

"There is, however, one thing I'd like you to do for me."

"Sure. What's that?"

"While I'm doing my preliminary investigation," he said, "I'd like you to put your own investigation on hold."

"Why?" I asked. I didn't see how what I'd been doing really qualified as an "investigation." I was only a high school student, after all, and it wasn't like I had anything more interesting going on. And despite Carolina's warning and Natalie's endorsement of Carolina's warning, I didn't see how continuing to play around on the Web was going to put me in danger.

"Please, humor me on this until we know more. All right, Delia?"

He was looking at me like he was waiting for a solemn promise, and I didn't want this to get in the way of his offer to help. "All right," I said.

He gave me his card and walked me to the door. "You just leave everything to me," he said as he shook my hand. "I'll be in touch soon."

I didn't know whether it was his kind smile or the dancing ponies or the simple fact that he was a sane adult who took me seriously, but I left his office in an exceptionally good mood. Even not knowing where I'd get the money to pay him seemed like a problem that would solve itself when the time came.

Out on the street, I wasn't about to waste what money I did have on a cab, so I checked the subway map I now carried everywhere to figure out how I could get back to the loft. And as I was returning the map to my bag, something made me look across the street and up, to where Rafe's office was.

The late-afternoon sun glanced off the glass, making it hard to tell, but I thought I could see him standing at his window, looking out. I wasn't sure if he could see me, but I smiled and waved.

It was reassuring to know he was there, like he was watching over me.

Twenty-one

When I got back to the loft, Charley was on the phone with Patience, which she signaled by using a finger and a thumb to mime shooting herself in the head. "Yes, I am listening," she was saying. "Yes, I understand it's important. . . . No, I'm not making any inappropriate gestures while I'm on the phone with you. . . . Yes, I will be sure to tell her. . . . No, she's not home yet, but I'll tell her when she gets here. . . . Okay . . . Good-bye . . . No, I won't forget. . . . Bye . . . Yes, bye. Bye."

She hung up and gave me a pained smile. "That was Patty."

"I figured."

"She's got a bee in her bonnet about Thaddeus J. Wilcox. I wonder how that saying ever got started? I mean, did anyone actually have a bee in his or her bonnet?"

"Was she able to get in touch with Thad?" I asked.

"No, and she's furious about it. Usually everybody jumps when she snaps, and there has been no jumping on his end. His end has been a jump-free zone. But his people are working with her people to get a teleconference on the calendar. She'll let you know when they schedule it. Personally, I don't have any people."

"I'll be your people," I offered.

"That is very kind of you," said Charley as the phone started to ring. "Ugh. If this is Patty again, will you pretend you're having an emergency of some sort? Nothing fatal or permanently scarring, but just enough of a crisis so I have an excuse to get off the phone?"

She picked up the call, and I started toward my room to change out of my uniform. But the way Charley's voice went from cautious to friendly and then filled with poorly suppressed excitement made me turn right back around. "Hello . . . No, this is her aunt. . . . May I ask who's calling? Oh! I mean, just a moment, please. I'll see if she's available."

She held the phone out toward me. "Quinn Riley," she said with an elaborate casualness that was completely at odds with the look of intense interest on her face.

I tried to compose myself and then took the phone from her. "Hello?" I said.

"Hey, Juliet. What's the deal?"

"What do you mean?" I asked. Charley didn't even bother to pretend that she wasn't listening, though she did make a big show of rifling through the pile of takeout menus on the counter.

"I mean, we've got this scene due on Monday but you keep cutting class. Which means we haven't even started rehearsing. And that would be fine except that the last thing I need right now is to flunk drama. I was counting on an easy A. I need something to offset my grade in calc."

"Oh, uh —"

"You know, if you don't want to do it, that's cool."

"No, that's not it —"

"I can get Mr. Dudley to cast someone else. I just need to know one way or the other."

This was a disaster, and meanwhile I was having a hard time thinking on my feet. To make matters worse, it wasn't like I could explain why I hadn't been in class or tell him how much I wanted to do the scene without then having to tell Charley why Quinn thought it was even an issue. And if I took the phone into my room for some privacy, that would only make her all the more curious.

"Hello?" Quinn asked. "You still there?"

"Okay. I'll see you then," I said, which was the best way I could think of to reassure him I'd be there tomorrow without letting Charley know that I hadn't been there today.

"So, you're in?"

"Yes," I said.

"You're sure?"

"I'm sure."

I hung up and handed the phone back to Charley. "Everything all right?" she asked. I might've set a dangerous precedent by telling her so much about Quinn already — now anything less than full disclosure must seem strange to her.

"Uh-huh," I said. "He just had a question he forgot to ask me today in class." She gave me a searching look, but I pretended not to notice and changed the subject to the one thing I knew would distract her. "What's for dinner?"

She fanned the menus in her hand. "I'm thinking either mac and cheese and *Sixteen Candles* or chicken pot pie and *St. Elmo's Fire*. What do you think?"

I thought it was getting hard to keep track of all of the things I couldn't let Charley know.

■　　■　　■

The next morning I told Natalie all about my meeting with Rafe. At this point, she was the only person I *could* tell. I expected her to be just as thrilled as I was, but she was bizarrely lukewarm. In fact, lukewarm was generous. It was more like suspicious. She was harder on him than she'd been on Carolina.

"So, he just called out of the blue and you don't know for sure how he got your number?" she said.

"He told me that someone I'd contacted had referred him to me. And it's not like he's a fake. He has an office and a license and everything," I said, trying not to sound defensive.

"Doesn't it seem a bit too convenient how he just sort of fell into your lap like that?" she asked. "And then he just offers to help you for free?"

"He's only doing a preliminary investigation for free. I'll have to pay him if he decides to take the case," I said, not that I had any idea how I was going to do that.

"Why does he want you to stop your own investigation?" she persisted. "Don't you think that's weird? Are you sure he's not connected with EAROFO or anyone else like that? What do you really know about this guy?"

She hadn't met Rafe, so she couldn't understand. I tried to figure out how best to explain him, searching for the right words as I watched people passing by on the sidewalk. It was an unremarkable parade of nannies taking kids to school, a dog-walker with a posse of Wheaton terriers, and all sorts of other Manhattanites starting their days. But then a woman walked by all dressed up in a business suit and trench coat and with her hair in a knot, and that reminded me.

"There were dancing ponies on his tie," I said. "What kind of bad guy would have ponies on his tie?"

For once, I'd stumped her. The first bell rang before she could come up with an answer.

Twenty-two

All day I still had that pleasant lightness I'd had since leaving Rafe's office, and I wasn't about to let Natalie spoil it, or even the pop quiz Ms. Seshadri sprang on us in pre-calc. And while part of it was because of Rafe, I'd be fooling myself if I didn't admit that the other part was from looking forward to seeing Quinn in drama.

After all, it was entirely possible that the reason he'd been back to his elusive ways on Monday had to do with how I'd run off on Saturday. And while it wasn't like he'd been declaring his undying love over the phone the previous night, the fact that he'd gone to the trouble to track down Charley's unlisted number said a lot. At least, I hoped it did.

But I was still a bit nervous about which Quinn I'd find when last period finally arrived. I was sitting on the edge of the stage, waiting for class to start, when he came over and sat down beside me. "Hey, Juliet," he said. "Glad you could make it."

I looked at him, wondering if he was being sarcastic. But he was smiling, and I couldn't detect even a hint of snarkiness, so I smiled back.

As soon as he'd finished taking attendance, Mr. Dudley gave us permission to go off on our own to rehearse our respective scenes.

Quinn turned to me. "Do you want to do this outside? We could go to the park."

"Sounds good," I said.

Central Park was less than a block away, and on our way there Quinn started telling me his ideas for the scene. "The obvious thing would be to play it straight, like we really were in sixteenth-century Verona, but that seems sort of tired. I was thinking that maybe we could set it in the present day instead. Nothing hokey, like on a spaceship or anything, but just having Romeo and Juliet be regular people, like us. We're not supposed to do costumes, so we'll be in our uniforms, but it would still be interesting to think through how we can deliver the lines and block it and everything to make it feel contemporary. What do you think?"

I thought he was surprisingly into this assignment for some-body who only cared about an easy A. And before I could stop myself, that's exactly what I said.

We were stopped at the corner, waiting for the light to change so we could cross Fifth Avenue. He smiled again and held a finger to his lips. "Shhh," he said. "Don't let anybody hear you say that. It's bad for my image."

"Do you care about your image?" Even as the words were coming out of my mouth I was mentally kicking myself. He'd been kidding around, and meanwhile I sounded like an after-school special. But he didn't seem to mind.

"Sure. It's my armor."

"Your what?" The WALK sign flashed, and he put a hand on my elbow as we crossed the street. And yes, even that faint pressure on that one small spot made my entire arm tingle.

"My armor. You know. Self-protective camouflage. Everybody has armor. Even you, I bet, though I still haven't figured out what form yours takes."

His tone was as light as always, but there was an undercurrent to his words that wasn't light at all. I wasn't sure how to respond, but my phone started ringing right as we reached the other side. The number on the screen was Rafe's.

"I'm really sorry," I said to Quinn. "This'll just take a second."

"Good news, Delia," said Rafe when I answered. "I contacted my source in Chile, and he reached out to his own network of sources. More than one reported hearing rumors of a ship-wrecked English-speaking couple hiding out in a remote area in Patagonia. It's a man and a woman, and descriptions of the woman match your description of your mother."

I tried to stay calm, but this was the first confirmation of T.K.'s whereabouts that wasn't based on assumptions about who might've made a phone call or the words of a Quik-swilling psychic. "Does anyone know where they are exactly? Is there any way to get in touch with them?"

"Remember, these are only rumors, but I trust my source, and he thinks his own sources are highly credible. I believe it's worth pursuing."

"Does that mean you'll take the case?" I asked.

"I'll take the case," he said. "In fact, I'd like to leave for Santiago as soon as possible. I'll just need a retainer to get started." Then he began reeling off his daily rates and explaining how I would also be responsible for reasonable and customary expenses and a lot of other things like plane tickets that sounded like they'd add up pretty quickly.

Yesterday's confidence that this was a problem that would solve itself when the time came started melting away in the presence of concrete numbers. I hadn't expected Rafe to work so fast — I'd thought I'd have more time to figure out how to pay him. And it was also becoming painfully clear that I'd significantly underestimated just how much it would all cost.

"I'm unable to accept credit cards, but as soon as I get your check, I can begin," Rafe was saying. "Twenty-five hundred should suffice for now."

It might as well have been twenty-five million, but I wasn't about to say that. I didn't want him to lose interest or momentum. "I'll get right on it," I said.

Quinn was watching my face when I got off the phone. "I think I know what your armor is," he said.

"Oh?" I asked, distracted. It was hard to concentrate on

anything else when all I could think was *twenty-five hundred dollars, twenty-five hundred dollars, twenty-five hundred dollars.*

"You remotely trigger a mysterious phone-based communication whenever you want to change the subject," said Quinn.

I had a credit card for emergencies and I could use it for a cash advance, but the bill went to Patience, and I was pretty sure the limit was too low to cover more than half of the retainer. I ran through a mental list of everyone I knew, even though I'd already been through the list countless times. Charley and Patience were out. It was too much to ask of Nora. Erin and Justin didn't have that kind of cash, and even if Natalie did and I was comfortable asking her, she wasn't about to let me spend it on Rafe.

"Or maybe you just don't want to talk to me," said Quinn.

His tone was still light, but when I looked up at him, his expression was serious. "No, that's not — I mean, I wasn't — it's not what you think —"

And that's when things turned into the cheesiest sort of after-school special: I started to cry. Even worse, this time there was nowhere to run.

"Hey, Juliet, what's going on?" Quinn asked, completely unfazed. And that made me cry harder.

He steered me over to a park bench and sat there with me, occasionally patting my back but otherwise just letting me go at it. He even produced a clean handkerchief from his pocket. I didn't know anyone still carried handkerchiefs.

I guess in a big city, people are used to seeing all sorts of things, so nobody who walked by seemed especially surprised to see me having a meltdown on a park bench. I even saw some of the same people as I'd seen that morning, like the dog-walker, though this time he had a herd of waddling pugs, and the woman in the trench coat, too.

Anyhow, none of them bothered us, and after ten minutes or so I was done. The reservoir hadn't had time to fully replenish itself since my last crying fit, but the emotional roller coaster I'd been on of late was wearing me out.

"You make Bea look like an amateur," said Quinn mildly.

"I've been practicing."

"I think you've nailed it," he said. "So, is there anything I can do? To help, I mean."

"Unless you know where I can find a big pile of cash lying around, probably not."

"As a matter of fact, I do," he said. "I won't even charge you interest."

"I was joking," I said.

"I wasn't," he said. And now his face was even more serious than it'd been when he was talking about my armor.

"Quinn, really. I'm talking about a lot of money."

"I have a lot of money. Hunter's a financial genius — he's minting the stuff. And whenever he feels guilty about exploiting the global energy crisis, he makes himself feel better by giving me more."

"But you can't just turn around and give it to me."

"Why not?"

"Because."

"Because what?"

"Just because."

"Okay, you cry better than Bea, but she'd totally crush you in a debate."

"I can't take your money."

"Look. Money's one thing I have. And I'm assuming you don't need it to support your drug habit or anything like that."

"No, nothing like that."

"Then what's the problem?" he asked.

"You hardly even know me."

He shrugged. "You saved my life. That jellyfish could've killed me."

"No it couldn't have and you know it."

"It's not like I earned it myself," he said. "I don't deserve it any more than anybody else does. But I have it, and if you don't use it, it will just sit there in the bank not doing anyone any good."

"But —"

"But what?"

On the one hand, it would have been so easy. On the other hand, there was something incredibly weird about feeling obligated to Quinn, especially given all of the other things I felt about him. But then again, maybe I was getting too used to everything being so hard.

"I'd pay you back," I said.

"I don't care. No strings attached." He spread his hands, palms up, as if to demonstrate the lack of strings.

"And you don't even want to know what it's for?" I asked.

"It's none of my business, is it?"

I looked at him and he looked at me. It was like jumping off a cliff, but without knowing what waited below or even how far it was to the bottom.

"Okay," I said, though I couldn't believe I was saying it. "If you insist."

Twenty-three

I ended up telling him anyway, and he even came with me to drop off the check. This time Rafe was wearing a tie with little giraffes on it, and I was tempted to take a picture to send to Natalie. I mean, first ponies and then giraffes? There was no way she could still be suspicious after that.

Rafe treated Quinn in the same kind, formal way he'd treated me and said he'd call when he had more news, though he warned it might not be until after the weekend. That felt sort of anticlimactic, but there was plenty to keep me busy in the meantime.

Thursday night I had go to Patience's for dinner. Charley was supposed to come, too, but she ended up being conveniently busy in the editing room and had to cancel at the last minute. I had a feeling she was actually curled up in her favorite chair back at the loft, eating ice cream and watching TV, but she'd already had to put in so much family time on my behalf that I couldn't blame her. Mostly I was just jealous.

Thanks to Carolina, I was now hyperconscious of the number eight, and I had to wonder what she would have made of

Patience's apartment. Not only was the address 888 Park Avenue, the apartment was on the eighth floor, and her foyer was painted a deep dark red.

But nothing inside felt dangerous. Everything looked like it had been decorated by Ralph Lauren, and a uniformed maid served us at a long table set with gold-rimmed china. This time I was careful to stay away from Gwyneth's water glass.

The conversation was about as stimulating as it had been in Southampton until Mr. Dudley came up. "He's such a talented young man," said Patience. "And so handsome. I was part of the search committee that hired him after the last drama instructor left. I'm so glad to hear he's working out."

A very slight tinge of color washed across Gwyneth's face, turning her complexion from white to off-white. In class, she'd been assigned a scene from *Our Town*. Apparently she'd be playing a dead person, but I seemed to be the only one at the table who found any humor in that. And Patience was thrilled to hear about Quinn and me doing *Romeo and Juliet*.

"So are you and Quinn an item, Delia?" she asked me.

"Excuse me?"

"You know, an item. Are you dating or hanging out or whatever it is that kids say these days?"

"Oh, uh, no," I said. "We're just friends." There was no way I was ever going to tell Patience how I really felt, and especially not at the dinner table with Jeremy and the Monkeys. And right then Gwyneth managed to knock over her father's wineglass, which created a welcome distraction. I was beginning to wonder if I'd been underestimating her.

It was raining on Friday, so Quinn and I couldn't go outside to rehearse and neither could anyone else. Which meant that the entire class was trying to rehearse in the auditorium. We ended up squeezed in a corner of the stage between a group doing a scene from *Death of a Salesman* and another group doing a scene from *Waiting for Godot*. It was a pretty hopeless situation. We couldn't even get all the way through our scene once without interruption, which meant we couldn't get to the kissing, either.

"What are you doing tomorrow?" Quinn asked, raising his voice to be heard over the din. "Do you want to come to my house and rehearse?"

Inside, I was dancing a happy mental jig, but I just said yes, of course, so that meant that Friday night Charley and I had to do outfit planning. It wasn't like I was going to wear my uniform to Quinn's apartment.

"Where does he live?" asked Charley.

I checked the address. "East Seventy-second Street?"

"I don't know why I asked. You do realize that you're probably the only person at Prescott who doesn't live on the Upper East Side? So we want put-together but a little funky." According to Charley, that meant a full-skirted dress from Anthropologie under a cropped cardigan with tights and Mary Janes, but she only decided on that after another prolonged session of trying on everything in my closet.

I took the subway uptown. I'd thought I'd finally gotten over feeling jittery about seeing Quinn, but the idea of doing our entire scene together, kiss and all, was enough to make the jitters come back with a vengeance.

The address belonged to a big stone building just off Fifth Avenue. One attendant held the door for me while another called to announce my arrival. Then a third took me up in an elevator that opened directly into the Rileys' apartment on the top floor.

Nobody was in the foyer, but I heard the sound of wheels on parquet and assorted thumps and yelps in the distance, so I headed in that direction. And a few wrong turns later, I found myself in what could really only be described as a ballroom.

It was the size of a regulation soccer field, with a wall of windows looking south over the city and an enormous crystal chandelier hanging from the ceiling, which had to be at least two stories high. And except for a grand piano in a corner, the entire space was practically empty.

Which made it perfect for Bea and Oliver's purposes. They were both wearing roller skates, and they'd set up an obstacle course using folded card tables and coatracks and even a miniature trampoline. They were gleefully bashing into walls and tables and each other like everything was made of rubber, including themselves.

"They're cute but not all that bright," Quinn said, coming up beside me as I watched.

"Delia!" Bea spotted me and zoomed over, with Oliver behind her. "Guess what we're doing."

"Practicing for your Mensa entrance exams?" suggested Quinn.

"Funny," said Oliver sarcastically. And then, "What's Mensa?"

"Delia, did you bring skates?" asked Bea, skating backwards in a circle around me. "You want to try our new Power Extreme Super Roller Challenge?"

"She'd love to some other time," said Quinn. "But we have homework to do. And don't you guys have to be somewhere?"

As if on cue, Fiona appeared in another of the ballroom's multiple doorways. "Beatrice! Oliver! How many times have I told you no skating in the house? I just had these floors refinished."

"So that's why it's extra slippery today," mused Oliver. "Cool."

Fiona herded them off to go change for somebody's birthday party, and Quinn led me through a few more rooms and into a small library.

We'd agreed the previous day that we would both have our lines memorized for today so that we could concentrate on how we actually wanted to say them. It wasn't like there was that much to learn — just the short dialogue between Romeo and Juliet. And thanks to Ash, I'd read the whole thing several times and seen it performed more than once. I already knew the scene pretty well.

But as much of the meaning was in what the characters did while they spoke — the blocking — as in the lines themselves, which played on the language of religious pilgrimage to justify first touching hands and then kissing. This was the hand-touching part that led to the kissing part:

ROMEO

If I profane with my unworthiest hand
This holy shrine, the gentle fine is this:
My lips, two blushing pilgrims, ready stand
To smooth that rough touch with a tender kiss.

JULIET

Good pilgrim, you do wrong your hand too much,
Which mannerly devotion shows in this;
For saints have hands that pilgrims' hands do touch,
And palm to palm is holy palmers' kiss.

So, while we were saying all this, we were touching our hands together, palm to palm. And this was obviously not the least nerve-wracking thing I'd ever done. Quinn seemed totally focused on the scene, and I was trying to focus, too, but the closer we got to the kissing part, the less easy that was. Either way, I was beginning to think that I liked drama. A lot.

Anyhow, we were almost up to the kissing part when somebody behind us cleared his throat and said, "Ahem."

I practically jumped out of my skin. A man was standing at the door watching us. And if I hadn't been blushing before, I was definitely blushing now.

But Quinn was completely calm. "Hey, Dad," he said. "This is Delia. Delia, this is my father."

"Hi, Mr. Riley," I said. After everything Charley had said and some of what Quinn had said, too, I was expecting a total ogre. But if Hunter Riley was an ogre, it didn't show on the outside. He looked like an older version of Quinn, though Quinn's hair was light brown where his father's was a much darker brown with some gray at the edges.

"Call me Hunter," he said. "What are you two up to?"

"Rehearsing," said Quinn. "We've got that drama class thing on Monday."

"That's right," said Hunter. "I'd forgotten about that. Is Marcus coming later?"

"Uh-huh," said Quinn.

"He said you should be able to bring your math score up to match your verbal score if you just work at it."

"Uh-huh," said Quinn again.

"I have some time before we go out this evening if you want to do a practice test with me," Hunter said.

"Okay," said Quinn.

"Good. Then I'll see you later. Nice to meet you, Delia."

"Nice to meet you, too," I said.

"That was Hunter," said Quinn as his father's footsteps faded away.

"I figured. Since he said to call him Hunter and everything."

"Marcus is tutoring me for the SATs. That's why Hunter was asking about him. He's very interested in improving my SAT scores."

"It shows," I said.

We went back to rehearsing, but the interruption had put a damper on things. Romeo and Juliet never had to worry about standardized tests. We started working everything over from the beginning, and it felt like it took forever to get back to the kissing part.

And then, just as we'd almost reached the moment, Fiona announced over an intercom that Quinn's tutor had arrived, and I decided I should probably go.

■　　■　　■

Saturday night I spent with Charley, who said it was too dangerous to leave the loft, not because of crime or anything but because it was "amateur night" in Manhattan. "The entire city's filled with — and forgive me for saying this, because it's the sort of thing Patty says — tourists and suburbanites. We're much better off staying here, where it's safe. Now, I'm thinking either *Reckless* and tapas or *Fire with Fire* and Korean barbecue."

But even Charley understood that a person can spend just so much time watching teen movie classics, so after we'd finished dinner, I let her think I was doing homework and went to spend some time online.

It was nice to know that Rafe was on the case, but it made me feel restless to just leave everything up to him. And in spite of all the people who'd been warning me about danger, I still didn't see how looking things up online from the loft was going to put me in harm's way. So I started Googling EAROFO's board of directors.

As major corporate executives, they were all public figures, so there was a ton of information available about each of them on their company Web sites and on Wikipedia. But I didn't find anything that conveniently mentioned how any of the executives was secretly trying to drill for oil in off-limits areas in Antarctica. I guessed that wasn't the sort of thing people tended to announce publicly.

What I really needed to do was talk to one of these executives myself, but with the exception of a company called Navitaco, none of their headquarters was in New York. But the Navitaco Web site did provide an e-mail address for contacting company management. So even though I knew it was a long shot, I composed an e-mail describing myself as a student working on an economics project and asked if I could schedule an interview with Leslie "Trip" Young, Navitaco's CEO. And just to be on the safe side, I sent it from my Delia Navare screen name.

Of course, it was Saturday night, so nobody got back to me. And I was still online, trying to figure out my next move, when an IM popped up. I was expecting Erin or Justin, reporting on their second date. They'd had plans to go to a solar observatory that afternoon, because to them the only thing more romantic than plate tectonics was looking at sunspots through a telescope.

But it was Quinn instead.

QUINNER: meet me tmrw? 1:45 pm, 365 W 49 St

That was cryptic. We'd discussed rehearsing more on Sunday, though we hadn't made a firm plan. But just seeing his IM up on the screen put an enormous, completely uncontrollable smile on my face.

DELIATRUE: ?
QUINNER: surprise. u in?

DELIATRUE: k

QUINNER: cool. c u there.

I stared at the screen for a long time after he'd logged out, still smiling uncontrollably, until Charley knocked to tell me she needed ice cream.

Twenty-four

Charley wasn't exactly a morning person, and she was proud of her ability to sleep through just about anything. She'd even slept through an elephant stampede back when she was in the Peace Corps. So when her home phone rang before seven A.M. on Sunday, she definitely wasn't going to answer it. Meanwhile, I didn't see why anyone would be calling for me on that line or that early in the day, so I wasn't rushing to grab it, either.

Out in the living room, the machine picked up the call and a female voice began leaving a message. The walls of my bedroom muffled the words, but I could hear well enough to tell from the woman's lilting tone that it wasn't my mother, which was the only thing that would've gotten me out of bed. So I rolled over and tried to go back to sleep.

But even Patience's tendency to fill up all of the space on the machine hadn't taught Charley to use the setting that limits the length of a message, so this message went on and on. And on and on and on. And then on some more.

I could hear the voice even with my pillow over my head, and unlike Charley, I couldn't sleep through anything. So then

I started counting, telling myself it would be over in thirty seconds. But after I'd counted to one hundred and the woman was still leaving her message, I crawled out of bed and went to answer the phone.

As soon as I opened the door of my room I recognized the voice. "— this dream, I am not sure what it will be meaning, but it is, how you say, a foretelling when I am having the dreams like this —"

I finally located the receiver under a pile of magazines and hit TALK. "Hello? Carolina?"

"This is Delia, *sí*? I cannot understand why you are not answering when I know you are in the house. Why are you being the ostrich with the pillow?" She sounded cranky, like I'd been deliberately ignoring her.

"I'm sorry," I said. "I just woke up. What was it you were saying about your dream?"

"In my country, the people have been up two, three hours already. You know, they are on the banana plantations, so they are working very hard to finish before it is too hot —"

I wasn't as bad as Charley, but that didn't mean I wanted to get up at the crack of dawn on a weekend to hear about agricultural practices in Ecuador. "That must be very demanding," I said politely. "Now, what was it you wanted to tell me about your dream?"

"I have the dream about the Sagittarius. Have you been not heeding my warning?"

"I'm a Pisces," I said.

"That is not what I said. The Sagittarius. He is dangerous for you."

"So I should stay away from anyone who's a Sagittarius?" I asked. That made more sense. Sort of.

"No, it is just the one Sagittarius. But I don't know who he is." I could hear the frustration in her voice. When you were used to knowing everything, it must be extra annoying when there was anything you didn't know. "It is bothering me a great deal — I cannot see it. But I am very sure that you have to be taking care with the Sagittarius. You understand?"

I promised her that I'd be careful, and she said she'd keep trying to figure out who, exactly, I needed to be careful of.

And while I knew enough by now to take any warning from Carolina seriously, it was hard to get too worked up that early in the morning or when the danger she'd described was so vague. I mean, one-twelfth of the people in the world had to be Sagittariuses, including Charley. Either way, I decided that the safest place for me just then was bed, so I went back to my room and slept until ten.

■   ■   ■

Charley and I had an extra-hard time figuring out what I should wear that afternoon, since we had no idea what Quinn had in mind. I ultimately headed out in an Anna Sui dress and boots and a bunch of Charley's gold bangles. "We need to do something about your lack of accessories," she said. "I've been sadly remiss. Maybe we can squeeze in some shopping one day this week."

Thanks to Carolina, I was on high alert for anything or anyone that seemed threatening, but it wasn't like you could tell when a person's birthday was just by looking at him. Out on the street it was a regular September day, and none of the people I saw seemed to be up to no good.

The subway took less time than I'd expected, and while the address Quinn had given me was in a part of the city I'd never been to before, I found it without any trouble. I even ended up getting there early, but I didn't think being early ruined the surprise. Though I couldn't be sure, because I couldn't figure out what was supposed to be surprising about the nondescript brownstone that matched the address.

I double-checked what I'd written down, and I definitely had the right number on the right street. The brownstone had been converted into several apartments, at least going by the number of buttons on the intercom panel, but Quinn hadn't given me an apartment number to ring. I'd have to wait until he got there.

He arrived right at 1:45, and just watching him walking down the street had me doing the uncontrollable smiling thing all over again.

"What's the surprise?" I asked, trying my best to act like someone who could control her facial expressions.

"Come on," he said, casually grabbing my hand, like holding hands on the street wasn't a big deal. "This address was a decoy. I didn't want the surprise to be ruined if you got here before me."

"Oh. That's very complicated," I said.

"I'm a complicated guy." He led me around the corner and down the next block. Then he stopped and pointed to a theater marquee across the street.

"Surprise," he said.

I was speechless.

"Well?" he asked. "What do you think?"

I looked up at him, and my words came back. "It's perfect," I said. "Absolutely perfect."

"I hope so. The tickets are nonrefundable."

He was taking me to see *Romeo and Juliet*.

■　■　■

It was a small theater, with maybe fifty seats, and the stage itself was tiny, so we were practically sitting on top of it. But the best part was that the production was by an experimental theater group, and they'd cast the play the same way it would've been cast in Shakespeare's day, with only four people playing all the roles, though one of the actors was a woman, which wouldn't have been allowed back then.

That meant that Romeo also played Juliet's mother, and Juliet also played Mercutio, and they both played multiple other roles, as did the two other actors. Each acted his or her individual parts so well that unless you really thought about it, you didn't even notice that you'd seen any of them in a different part just seconds earlier.

"This is amazing," I said to Quinn at intermission.

"It is sort of cool, isn't it?" he said. "And it's good to see you not stressing for once."

"I'm not always stressing," I protested as we made our way to the lobby.

He didn't say anything — all he did was raise one eyebrow.

"What's that supposed to mean?" I asked.

"I didn't say anything."

"You did the one-eyebrow thing."

"What one-eyebrow thing?" he asked, raising his other eyebrow.

"You've only seen me under unusual circumstances," I said. "Usually I'm totally carefree. It's just hard not to stress with everything I've got going on right now."

"Isn't that what the detective's for? To handle of all that?"

"In a way. But there are still things I can be doing while Rafe is doing his thing."

"What things?" asked Quinn. So I told him about researching the directors of EAROFO and trying to figure out how I could talk to one of them.

"Are you sure that's a good idea?" he said. "I mean, don't you suspect these people of going after your mom?"

"That's why I need to try to find out more."

"But what's to keep them from going after you?"

He was the second person that day to warn me, but he didn't have Carolina's special skills. "As far as anyone knows, I'm a harmless high school student — that's why I used my dad's name," I said. "And what could they do to me anyway? As long as I'm careful not to be alone with anyone dangerous. I mean, you can't exactly make a person disappear when she's surrounded by other people."

"If we were in a movie, right now they'd cut to somebody making you disappear," said Quinn.

"It's not a movie. But if I'm not back from the ladies' room in five minutes, you can call the police, okay?"

There was only one other person in the bathroom, a woman about Charley's age with shoulder-length brown hair, and she didn't exactly radiate danger. I had to wait for her to finish washing her hands before I could wash mine, and it was such a small space that it seemed awkward not to say anything. So I asked her if she was enjoying the play.

"What?" she said, like I'd startled her. And I probably had — I was always forgetting that people in New York weren't automatically friendly the way they were in California. She moved aside and I stepped up to the sink.

"The play. Are you enjoying it?"

"Oh, uh, yeah," she said, ducking her head to find something in her purse.

"I hope the second half is as good as the first," I said.

She mumbled something and left, and I dried my hands and followed her out.

■　■　■

The second half was just as good as the first, and maybe even better, though I embarrassed myself by tearing up during the death scene. Quinn probably thought I had some sort of compulsive crying disorder on top of my split personality, inability to stop stressing, and various other psychological problems.

But if he did, he didn't seem to mind.

Because he held my hand all the way through the rest of the play, right up to the curtain calls.

Twenty-five

If I'd thought things were awkward in the ladies' room, that was nothing compared to the awkwardness after the play. Not immediately, but when we were saying good-bye.

"Can I put you in a cab?" Quinn asked outside the theater.

"Oh, no. I'll take the subway. I like the subway." I was getting proud of my subway mastery. Besides, Charley said cabs were for tourists.

"Really?" said Quinn. "I didn't think Prescott girls were allowed to take public transportation."

"I've had all my shots," I told him.

"Then I'll walk you to the station."

"You don't have to," I said.

"I want to. This isn't the safest neighborhood. My mother once got mugged not far from here."

It was still light out, and while it might not have been the Upper East Side, it looked pretty safe to me, but I wasn't about to turn him down. And this was the first time I'd ever heard him talk about his mother. "Was she hurt?" I asked as we walked down the block.

"No, more just shaken up. It was a long time ago, before my parents split up, but I remember it because she was so freaked out. She was sort of" — he chose his words carefully — "emotionally delicate to start with, so it didn't take much to upset her."

"Oh," I said, not sure what else to say.

And that's when the awkwardness started.

"Yeah, well, here we are," Quinn said abruptly. We'd reached the subway entrance, and a train must have just arrived, because people started streaming out and we were suddenly in the middle of a crowd.

"Thank you," I said, as a group of tourists in matching I ♥ NY sweatshirts threatened to sweep us along toward Times Square. "This was really perfect."

"I'm glad you liked it," said Quinn. "And I think we're ready."

"What? Oh. I hope so." With all the hand-holding and then the thing about his mother and now wondering how we were going to part ways — would there be kissing? — I'd almost forgotten that we were doing our scene in class the next day.

"So, I guess I'll see you tomorrow," he said.

"Yes. Tomorrow."

"Okay, then."

"Okay," I echoed. "Bye."

"Bye," he said.

And that was it. I waited one more awkward moment, but nothing happened, and definitely not kissing. I just went down the stairs to the subway and caught an express train to Canal Street.

■ ■ ■

Charley beat me out of the loft on Monday morning. Gertrude had found a graphic designer that she insisted was the only possible choice for the film credits, but Charley didn't trust her judgment. "Let's just say that Helga's aesthetic sense leaves a lot to be desired," she said. Which meant that Charley had set up a full day of meetings with other designers, and she rushed off before I was even dressed.

Meanwhile, I hadn't heard anything from Rafe, and nobody had e-mailed me back from Navitaco, but Quinn grabbed me on my way into my first-period class.

"Hey," he said, so casually that I wondered if he felt any of the awkwardness I'd felt the previous day. Maybe someone like Quinn was immune to that sort of thing. "I had an idea after I got home last night. Why don't you talk to my dad? His fund invests in different types of energy businesses — he probably knows all about the companies you're interested in and what they're up to. And that way you don't have to worry about the entire spider-and-fly situation."

"Excuse me?"

"You know. 'Come into my parlor, said the spider to the fly.' And then the spider eats the fly."

"Am I the spider or the fly in this scenario?" I asked.

"You're the fly, obviously. And these oil company execs are the spiders. So, I'd rather you talk to Hunter than get caught in their web."

"That almost makes sense," I said.

"Then I'll set it up," he said.

"Wait, Quinn," I said. "Don't tell your dad the whole thing, okay? Could you do what I did when I sent out the e-mail to the guy at Navitaco and just tell him I'm working on a project? And could you use my middle name, and not my last name?"

He smiled. "What, are you worried about Hunter?"

"No, of course not. But if he knows all these companies and everything, it just seems like it would be best."

He shrugged. "Okay. I'm on it. See you later, Juliet." And then he was gone.

■　■　■

Natalie had been out on Friday, on a three-day weekend of college visits with her parents, but she was eager to catch up during lunch. And after I heard more than I'd ever wanted to know about the undergraduate science programs at MIT, Harvard, and Cornell, I brought her up-to-date on everything that had been going on with me.

Of course, being Natalie, she was only mildly curious about Quinn. She was much more interested in what Rafe had to say and his trip to Chile.

"Does this mean that you trust Rafe now?" I asked. "Was it the giraffes that changed your mind?"

"No, I'm still not sure if I trust him and even if I did, it wouldn't be because of the giraffes," she said, like I'd insulted her by suggesting it. "That would be like trusting him based on his favorite flavor of Pop-Tart or whether he can ice-skate his astrological sign or something ridiculous like that."

"Do you think signs are ridiculous?"

She looked at me like I should have known the answer to that without asking.

So then I told her about Carolina and the Sagittarius warning. "I mean, Carolina's been so right about everything that it's hard to ignore her advice, but I don't know what to make of this one. But if you don't believe in Carolina and you don't believe in astrology, then you probably don't think it's important."

"I'm a Sagittarius. Maybe you should be watching out for me," she said dryly. "And centaurs, too. There aren't a lot of them at Prescott, but you never know when one might decide to canter into precalc."

"Why centaurs?"

"That's the symbol of Sagittarius — half man, half horse, with a bow and arrow. And their element is fire and their birthstone is topaz, so you should probably also watch out for any fire-breathing, topaz-wearing archery enthusiasts. Could I borrow your notes from physics on Friday, by the way? Or did you not take any?"

⬛   ⬛   ⬛

It didn't even hit me until I was on my way to drama, and then it wasn't the fire or the topaz. I realized that I hadn't seen centaurs recently but I had seen horses — at least, I'd seen the dancing ponies on Rafe's tie.

Did that mean I should actually be suspicious of Rafe, just like Natalie was? And did ponies even count as full-fledged horses? Rafe had been wearing that tie days before Carolina's Sagittarius warning — but maybe it was grandfathered in somehow?

Either way, that's what I was thinking when I got to drama, which was probably a good thing, because otherwise I'd have been completely freaking out about getting up on stage and doing the scene with Quinn, instead of just partially freaking out. And when Quinn sat down next to me and said, "Game on," I had no idea what he was talking about.

"Which game?"

"My dad will see you right after school. At his office."

"Seriously? Just like that?"

"Well, not quite. I had to agree to an extra session of SAT prep with Marcus, so I won't be able to go with you. Is that okay? Will you be all right on your own?"

I doubted that Charley would be terribly happy about my

going off to meet Hunter Riley unaccompanied, but I wasn't going to tell Quinn that, and I also didn't see what harm it could do. "I'll be fine," I said as Mr. Dudley called us to order.

He made us all sit in a circle and do the usual set of breathing exercises, which gave me an opportunity to do the full-on freaking out that I hadn't done earlier. By the time the exercises were over and everyone but Quinn and me had been shooed off the stage and into the first few rows of seats, I was more nervous and self-conscious than I'd realized was possible. And the modest high school auditorium seemed enormous, like I couldn't possibly make my voice fill the vast space.

"Whenever you're ready, people," said Mr. Dudley from the front row.

"Ready?" Quinn asked me.

I didn't feel like I'd ever be ready, but I nodded and turned to face him.

And that's when it happened.

I put my palm against his, and he began to speak his first line, and suddenly it was like I wasn't there.

I was Juliet and Quinn was Romeo, and the lines weren't dead black-and-white words on a page but somehow alive, as natural and real as the argument we'd had about the spider and the fly. The rows of empty seats were gone, and we were in a candlelit ballroom, wrapped in our own cocoon of words. But the playful banter of our words couldn't mask what we both knew — that after this, nothing would be the same.

And then we got to the kissing part, which we'd only read through together and had never really rehearsed. But it didn't matter, because I was still Juliet and Quinn was still Romeo, his gray-green eyes fixed on mine. And when he bent to kiss me, it was Romeo's lips on Juliet's.

Even so, Juliet was just as stunned as I would've been. When I said my last line, I was speaking for both of us. *You kiss by the book.*

Twenty-six

I was so caught up in the whole thing that it took me a second to realize we'd finished. The auditorium was completely silent.

Then, after an interminable moment, a girl in the second row began to clap, and then another, and then everyone was clapping — even Mr. Dudley.

And the clapping was almost as good as the kissing.

Actually, that wasn't even close to true. The kissing was much, much better.

■ ■ ■

I took the bus down Fifth Avenue from school to Quinn's father's office in Midtown. I should have spent the ride thinking about what I wanted to ask him, but mostly I was still stuck on the kissing. I mean, did it count as kissing if it occurred in the context of a play? If so, then I'd just had my first real kiss. But I wasn't sure it counted.

Hunter Riley's office was in a shiny glass tower on the edge of Bryant Park, opposite the New York Public Library. There was a reception desk in the lobby, and the man there found my name on a list of expected visitors after I showed him my school

ID. "Take the express elevator up to forty," he said, handing me a pass and pointing out which elevator bank to use.

A woman was waiting when the elevator doors slid open on the fortieth floor. She wore a pale blue suit and clunky gold jewelry, with the same carefully styled hair and perfect lipstick that newscasters have on TV. "You must be Delia!" she said, with far more enthusiasm than really seemed necessary. "I'm Kimberly, Mr. Riley's assistant. He's looking forward to seeing you."

She led me through a maze of cubicles filled with serious-looking men and women, all peering intently at their computer screens. Hunter Riley was at the far end of the floor, in a large glassed-in office with a view over the city skyline.

He was pacing and talking into a headset, but he waved me in with a big smile, indicating a chair across from his desk and gesturing that he'd be off the phone soon. "That's it," he was saying. "Five thousand October puts at the three-fifty strike price . . . set up a synthetic hedge to offset the position . . . got it?"

I'd just noticed the silver-framed photos of Quinn and Bea and Oliver on a credenza when he ended his call. "Delia, welcome," he said with another big smile. "Now, what can I do for you? Quinn said you had a project you wanted my advice about?"

"It's an independent study," I said, which was sort of true. "About variables affecting global oil supply and demand."

"Well, you've come to the right place. That's what I do — essentially, I make bets on what's going to happen to the prices of different commodities, and oil's my specialty."

What followed was a half-hour lesson about the different stocks and bonds and other types of securities you can use to buy and sell oil. I pretended to understand, and I even took notes, but he might as well have been speaking Mandarin. He was also so genuinely thrilled that somebody was taking an interest in his job that it seemed wrong to interrupt him.

When he eventually paused, I tried to steer him back toward the questions I actually wanted answered. "What would happen if somebody suddenly found a big new oil supply? Prices would go down, right?"

"Exactly," he said. "When supply goes up, prices go down, and vice versa. The tricky part is that prices already reflect what people know about future oil supply — it's well-documented where the oil is and who's pumping it. So if you want to make money, you need to have better information, so you can have a different opinion than everyone else and be right about it."

"How do you get better information?"

"Oh," he said vaguely. "Research. You know, talking to people in the business."

"Like the oil companies?" I asked.

"Sure. There are rules about what they can tell you, but you can learn a lot if you drill — I mean, dig."

"What if they're doing something they're not supposed to?"

"What do you mean?"

"Like secretly drilling in a place that's off-limits."

He shifted in his seat. "That's pretty complicated. And I'm afraid I have to jump on another call in a moment. But maybe we can discuss it some other time."

Kimberly buzzed through to let him know his 5:30 call was holding for him, and before I knew it, Hunter was escorting me out of his office. "It was good to see you again, Delia. I wish Quinn was as interested in what I do as you are. Kimberly, will you see Miss Truesdale out?"

I barely even had a chance to thank him. He already had his headset back on. "Right," he was saying. "Right, right. The October puts. Got it, Trip."

■   ■   ■

Kimberly waited with me until a down elevator arrived. "Bye now!" she said, with just as much enthusiasm as she'd used to greet me.

I pushed *L* for the lobby, and the elevator began its descent, but this time I wasn't taking the express. On thirty-nine, a bike messenger got on, still wearing his hat and with his iPod cranked so loud I could identify what was playing (Jay-Z). On thirty-five, we picked up a guy in a pinstripe suit. He smelled like smoke, and he had a cigarette and lighter in his hand, like he didn't want to waste a second once he got outside. Then, on thirty-three, the doors slid open and a woman in a trench coat walked in.

I was busy thinking about what I'd learned from Quinn's dad, and the doors slid shut before the company name on the reception desk could fully register. And fortunately, the woman was occupied with her BlackBerry — her head was down, and her thumbs were busy on the tiny keypad, so I didn't think she noticed me at all. I slipped behind the guy in the pinstripe suit, just in case, and I made sure to let the woman walk well ahead of me on the way out. This was easy, since my knees were shaking. I actually felt faint, and it wasn't a delayed reaction to kissing Quinn.

It's possible I was overreacting, and that it was all a coincidence, but I didn't think so.

Because the company on the thirty-third floor was Navitaco. And the woman in the trench coat was the same woman I'd seen walking past Prescott, and in Central Park, and, I realized belatedly, in the ladies' room at *Romeo and Juliet*. Today she was wearing her hair loose again, which was what made me put it together.

Meanwhile, Quinn had assured me he'd told his dad I was Delia Navare, but Hunter had distinctly referred to me as "Miss Truesdale." And no matter how I tried to tell myself it wasn't possible, I just couldn't shake the conviction that Hunter's 5:30

call had been with Leslie "Trip" Young, the Navitaco CEO and EAROFO director.

But the biggest part of the coincidence didn't even occur to me until the elevator doors opened on the ground floor. When Carolina had been warning me about a Sagittarius, had she actually been warning me about an archer? Because with his bow and arrow, an archer was a type of hunter.

And the only hunter I knew was Hunter Riley.

Twenty-seven

I was still trying to connect the dots when I got back to the loft, but they refused to line up in any recognizable way — or, at least in a way that would make Quinn's father unconnected to all of the people I suspected of being up to no good. And it didn't help that there'd still been no word at all from Rafe. So when Charley burst through the door, demanding a complete account, it took me a second to remember she was talking about the scene in drama.

"And?" she prompted, when I'd told her Mr. Dudley had seemed pleased.

"And what?" I said.

"You made it through the entire scene?" she asked.

"Sure. Didn't I tell you that?"

"Then aren't you leaving out something important?" she said.

"Huh?"

"Are you being dense on purpose?" she said.

"Is that a nice thing to say?" At this point I knew exactly what she was getting at, but it was sort of fun holding out, and I was in desperate need of fun.

"Did you *kiss* him?" she said, totally exasperated.

"Oh. Oh, right. Yes."

"And how was it?"

If she'd asked me right after it had happened, I probably would've done a better job of describing it. But now, instead of just wondering whether it counted as a kiss if it happened in a play, I was worrying about what it meant if it came from someone whose father might be trying to destroy your mother.

■ ■ ■

After dinner, I told Charley I had homework and settled myself on my bed with a pad of paper and a pen. Of course, homework was pretty much the last thing I intended to do. Mostly what I wanted was to curl up with a gallon of ice cream and a spoon and watch a lot of mindless TV. If Carolina thought my head had been noisy before, she'd be totally awed by how noisy it was now. And there was no escape, at least not unless I was up for a lobotomy or quickly developing a serious substance abuse issue.

T.K. always says that the best way to "create order out of chaos" is to put things down on paper. For her, this means an elaborate PowerPoint document with headings and subheadings and complicated graphs, but I didn't know how to use PowerPoint, so I just made a list. Here's what I came up with:

- Bad guys — EAROFO and maybe Quinn's dad — are illegally trying to extract oil from the Ross Sea.

209

- T.K. found out and went to investigate — but she didn't want Thad to know the details.
- The bad guys found out about T.K. and went after her.
- Somebody — the bad guys or maybe even T.K. herself — orchestrated the *Polar Star*'s disappearance.
- T.K. escaped to Chile to hide out.
- Thad was trying to take over her company.
- I haven't heard from Rafe since he left for Chile.
- Nobody responded to my e-mail to Navitaco, but a woman who worked there keeps showing up wherever I do and Quinn's dad might be doing business with them.
- I have to beware of a Sagittarius — and while Rafe dresses like one, Quinn's dad is named like one.
- The only people I can talk to about the whole thing are a skeptical teenage genius, a psychic, a private detective who might be dangerous, and Quinn, who may or may not have given me my first kiss and whose father might or might not be one of the bad guys.

I looked over what I'd written. But even with PowerPoint, I still wouldn't have been able to make order out of this chaos, let alone figure out what to do next. And when I called Natalie, who was pretty much the only person I could turn to if I wanted to talk it all through, she was so busy with a project for a citywide science fair that her parents wouldn't let her stay on the phone for long. She had just one thing to say:

"This is serious stuff. You should be very, very careful."

■　■　■

Tuesday started out gray and rainy, which fit right in with my mood. I still hadn't heard from Rafe, and his phone was going straight to voice mail. I'd come up with and then discarded hundreds of things to say to Quinn, but it was impossible to know how I should act when I didn't know if the kiss had meant anything, if his father was evil, or if he knew that his father was evil. Meanwhile, enough people had warned me about danger enough times that paranoia had begun to set in.

On my way to school, I put to use every tactic I'd ever seen in a movie to identify and lose a tail. I paused at store windows, looking for familiar faces reflected in the glass. I sped up and slowed down to see if anyone else was matching my pace. I stopped to tie my shoes, checking to see if other people stopped behind me. I even stepped into a subway car and then jumped out again just before the doors closed.

I felt a bit silly doing all this, but it wasn't like anyone was watching. Which was what I proved with the evasion tactics — nobody was following me or lying in wait or anything like that. So that was reassuring, though I still couldn't help but feel completely on edge.

The day seemed to pass in a blur. Mostly I kept pulling out my list whenever I had a chance, hoping it would suddenly morph into a clear course of action. I didn't see Quinn all morning, but that was sort of a relief given my confusion about what I'd say to him. And when Gwyneth came over to talk to me at lunch, it was just another surreal event in a long chain of surreal events.

"Hi," she said, taking a long pull of Tab.

"Hi," I said.

"It was really good yesterday. In drama. The scene you did with Quinn."

"Oh. Thanks."

"What's going on with you two anyhow?"

"What do you mean?" I asked, almost too shocked by the fact that she'd initiated a conversation to process what she was saying.

"I mean, are you together?"

Even if I'd wanted to, I wouldn't have known how to answer that. And as far as I could tell, she was going out with the guy I'd seen her with at the party, so I couldn't figure out why she was asking.

"Uh, we're friends, I guess," I said as Natalie seated herself opposite me. And Gwyneth was either satisfied by my answer or she didn't want to be seen in such close proximity to an overachiever like Natalie, because she strolled away.

By the time last period arrived, my edginess had grown into

an allover feeling of intense unease, and it didn't help that there was still no word from Rafe. I'd spotted Quinn on his landing after lunch, hanging out with Grey and Gwyneth and some of the other Alliance members, but that seemed like too much to handle, so I pretended I hadn't seen him. And when I got to drama, he was already sitting between two other seniors, so I took a seat in another row to watch the scenes that other kids were doing that day.

But when the bell rang at the end of class, Quinn materialized at my side.

"Hey, what are you up to now?" he asked. His voice sounded deliberately casual, but it still had its usual effect on me.

"Um," I managed to get out.

"Want to grab coffee or something and talk?"

"Uh, sure."

"Cool. I'll meet you out front in ten minutes."

I went to collect my things from my locker, wondering the entire way what Quinn wanted to talk about. As a general rule, any conversation that started with some form of the statement "we should talk" ended in a breakup — at least that's how it worked on TV. But Quinn and I weren't even going out, were we?

He wasn't there yet when I got outside, but the seniors had their own lounge, and that's where their lockers were — I figured he'd probably run into a bunch of people and stopped to talk. I waited on the steps for him to show up.

The rain had stopped, but it was still gray out. It felt sort of like San Francisco. The air was moist, and there was even fog, though nowhere near as thick as it was at home.

Five minutes went by, and then ten. When I'd first come out, there'd been a stream of students leaving the building. But at this point, anyone who wasn't staying for an extracurricular had pretty much left. I was also starting to get chilled, which only added to the unease, so I began pacing back and forth on the sidewalk.

After fifteen minutes, I was thinking about going inside to track down Quinn — I mean, I might've been confused, but I didn't think he would completely stand me up — when a woman called my name from across the street. "Delia."

I turned in the direction of her voice. It was the woman from Navitaco, and the play, and the park.

"Delia," she called again, waving me toward her with both hands. "I have a message for you."

I moved closer to the curb, keeping an eye on her hands to make sure she wasn't holding a weapon of any sort and reaching into my bag so I had my phone at the ready. "What kind of message?" I asked. "Who are you?"

"Come here," she said. "I'll tell you."

I was a bit offended that she'd think I was that stupid. "No, thank you," I said. I was much happier where I was, with the street safely between us and the shelter of the school at my back and the occasional pedestrian or car passing by.

"Delia, it's important," she said.

"Then tell me from over there —" I was starting to say when I heard a car come speeding down the street, way faster than cars are supposed to go in a school zone. Or any other sort of zone, for that matter. I automatically turned my head at the sound.

The black SUV was ten yards away when it jumped the curb. And instead of braking or swerving, it accelerated and headed straight for me.

Twenty-eight

Surfing teaches you balance, but it's also good for reflexes and agility. I lunged away from the SUV, throwing myself up and onto the steps.

It barreled past, glancing off a fire hydrant and back into the street without losing speed. Then there were running footsteps from behind me, and Quinn sprinted by in a blur of motion, yelling and chasing after the car. But it had too much of a head start. It disappeared around the corner and merged with the traffic on Fifth Avenue.

He ran back to where I was sprawled on the steps.

"You okay?" he asked, kneeling beside me.

"I think so." I had a shallow cut from where a piece of the SUV's fender had grazed my shin, and my hip and torso were sore from where they'd hit the hard stone. And I was terrified, but that didn't count as physical damage.

I struggled up into a sitting position and looked across the street. The woman in the trench coat was gone.

■ ■ ■

A teacher inside had heard the noise and called the police. They arrived almost instantly, and I told them everything I remembered. I didn't know what make or model the SUV was, though Quinn thought it might have been a Range Rover, and he'd also caught two numbers off its license plate. Neither of us had gotten a good look at the driver, nor had the entire incident been in range of the school's security cameras.

The policeman in charge said it had probably been someone driving under the influence of alcohol or drugs who'd lost control of the car. Of course, he hadn't been there to see it speeding up as it headed straight at me. Nor did he seem optimistic about tracking down the driver, given the number of black SUVs in Manhattan on any given day and the lack of more information.

The school nurse was still in the building, and somebody went to get her. She came out and took a look at my shin and then gently poked at the area where I felt bruised. One of her gentle pokes hurt so much, I couldn't help but give a little yelp, but even if she hadn't insisted, Quinn would have made me go to the emergency room to get checked out.

Charley met us there, and it all took forever, but eventually I was X-rayed and diagnosed with a cracked rib. And there was nothing the doctor could do but tape it up, give me a pain-killer, and advise me to avoid coughing and hiccups, like anybody had any control over hiccups. I couldn't even stop the shaking that had started the second the SUV was gone.

Charley went out to wait with Quinn while the doctor was finishing up, and when I eventually joined them in the reception area, it looked like the cracked rib was going to be the least of my problems. Even facing a moving vehicle intent on mowing me down hadn't been as scary as the look on Charley's face.

"I can take it from here," she said to Quinn. "Thank you for everything."

"Are you sure I can't help get her home?" he asked, like I wasn't even there.

Charley spoke before I could. "That's sweet of you, but we'll manage on our own. Thanks again." And she swept me out of the emergency room and into a cab before I could say anything to Quinn myself.

"Fifteen Laight Street, please," she told the driver. Then she turned to me. "How are you doing?" she asked.

"Okay," I said, though it came out a little wobbly.

"Does it hurt?"

"No. The doctor gave me a painkiller."

"Are you sure you're all right?"

"Really. I'm fine."

"Then would you like to hear about my day?" she asked.

"Uh, sure," I said.

"Well, first, I spent many, many tedious hours in the editing room with Dieter and Helga. Then I dragged myself home, where I noticed that there was a message on the answering machine. And when I pressed PLAY, I got to hear Carolina

Cardenas going on and on about how you're in danger before she was suddenly cut off."

"Oh," I said. "Whoops." I'd forgotten that Carolina must have left several minutes' worth of message before I'd picked up the other morning.

"Yes, whoops. Now, as I'm sure you can imagine, I found that somewhat worrying, so I picked up the phone to call you. But before I could dial your number, Quinn called to inform me that you're in the emergency room after a narrow escape from attempted vehicular homicide."

"Uh —" I started, but she was on a roll.

"I arrived in the emergency room to find you bloodied and broken —"

"There wasn't that much blood, and it's only a cracked —"

"And as I waited for you to be put back together, I got to hear from Quinn all about your recent extracurricular activities, including how you've financed them, as well as his own assessment of the danger to which you are exposing yourself. And now I just have one question for you. Do you know what that question is?"

"Uh —"

"WHY DID YOU NOT TELL ME ANY OF THIS YOURSELF?" she exploded. Even the driver turned around to look.

"I couldn't," I said.

"Why not?"

"Because you thought I was suffering from an 'understandable reluctance to meet reality head-on' and Patience was ready to have me committed."

She was silent for what felt like an endless moment. "I should probably give you a lecture on eavesdropping, but God knows I did plenty of it when I was your age. I do wish you'd talked to me about it, though, because you've created a lot of drama where there didn't need to be any. If I'd known you wanted a detective to investigate things more thoroughly, I would have arranged for it."

"You wouldn't have thought I was crazy?"

"Of course not. Even if I didn't agree with you, I could understand why you'd want to make sure no stone had been left unturned or whatever the right metaphor is. And from what Quinn told me, it sounds like you're on to something."

"I think I am," I said.

"But here's what's going to happen. I'm going to talk to your detective, and I'll be in charge of things from now on. And you are going to stop whatever you've been doing and start acting like a regular high school student, or as regular as someone can be when they have to go to Prescott. Because I really, really don't want to have to worry about you being run over or anything like that ever again. Do you understand?"

"I understand," I said.

"Good," she said. Then she exhaled a long breath and leaned

back in her seat. "I can't believe I just talked to you like that. Ugh. I sounded like someone's mother." She said "mother" like she was talking about cockroaches or snakes.

"It was pretty impressive," I said. "I never would have guessed you were an amateur."

We were both silent for a bit as the cab made its way through traffic. Then Charley spoke again. "Look," she said. "Not to get all soppy and everything, though it's probably already too late for that, but I'm figuring this whole thing out in real time. So if you think I'm not getting it right, you need to let me know. Patience wasn't completely wrong. That Chia Pet did die on my watch, and you're the first living creature anyone's trusted me with since. And sometimes I do wonder what your mother was thinking — the last time she saw me, I was ten and throwing a fit because Old Addie wouldn't let me wear my Batgirl outfit to her college graduation. But for whatever reason, she trusted me with you. I'm doing my best not to betray her trust, and I promise to do my best not to betray yours, either. Okay?"

"Okay," I said.

She exhaled another long breath. "So, now that we've got that settled, I'm thinking it might make sense to skip dinner and go straight to ice cream. How does that sound to you?"

Twenty-nine

The painkiller the doctor gave me in the emergency room started to seriously kick in soon after we arrived at the loft, and I was too tired to stay up even for ice cream. I barely remembered getting into bed, and I definitely didn't remember falling asleep, but I woke up a little after midnight. My side throbbed a bit, but mostly I was thirsty. And when I thought about getting a glass of water, my limbs felt too heavy to possibly move.

The door to my room was ajar, so I could hear Charley in the living room. She was on the phone, speaking in a low voice.

I called her name, but my throat was so dry it came out sort of whispery. Then I tried again, and she still didn't hear me. But I could hear bits and pieces of what she was saying.

"... tomorrow ... does she ... tell her ... so disappointed ... best option ... secure enough ... the risk is ... the right time ... now that we know ..."

I wanted to hear more, but the medicine was pulling me under again, despite the thirst. My eyes closed, and when I

222

opened them again, the sun was streaming in and I was definitely late for school.

■ ■ ■

When I came out of my bedroom, Charley was sitting at the round table with the phone and a cup of coffee, flipping through the pages of a magazine.

"What are you doing?" she asked in surprise when she saw me all dressed in my uniform. "You don't have to go to school today. That's the silver lining to this whole thing. You've missed the entire morning anyway. You might as well miss the afternoon, too."

"I want to go," I told her. "Otherwise I'll just be sitting around waiting to hear from Rafe and losing my mind."

"Oh. I wanted to talk to you about that. You did hear from him," she said.

"I did?"

"Last night, while you were sleeping. I hope you don't mind — I answered your phone — it was so late that I didn't think anyone would call unless it was important."

"No, that's fine. What did he say?" I asked eagerly.

"Do you want anything to eat?" she asked.

"I'm not hungry. What did he say?" I asked again.

"He was catching a flight out of Santiago, but he said he'd call when he landed in New York this evening."

"That's all?"

"Well, no. We discussed it and agreed it made sense to suspend his investigation at this point. That's why he's coming back. Are you sure you don't want anything to eat?"

"What do you mean, suspend?" I asked.

"We decided that we needed to, uh, regroup."

"Regroup?" My voice was suddenly coming out an octave higher than usual. "I don't need to regroup. None of us need to regroup. We need him to find T.K. and figure out what's going on so that she can come home."

"Delia, Rafe was very distressed to hear about what happened last night, and right now the most important thing is to make sure you're safe. That's why we need to take a step back and —"

"So you called him off."

"No, that's not it. Rafe agreed with me about this — it was actually his idea —"

"Rafe's idea?"

"Yes," said Charley.

But — how could Rafe stop investigating now? How could the investigation be at an end if he hadn't found T.K.?

There was an obvious answer to that question. But I refused to even form the words in my head.

Because it couldn't be true. It couldn't.

There was a ringing noise in my ears again, and the floorboards seemed to sway beneath my feet.

"Delia, listen to me, this is the best course. Just wait until Rafe gets back and you can talk to him —"

The rest of her words faded away, because I'd already grabbed my bag and my phone and was running out the door.

From the moment Thad and Nora told me about T.K., the stress and confusion and general feeling of being lost had been a constant, always there in the same way that I knew my own name — even when good things were happening, like kissing Quinn. The only thing holding me together had been my confidence that my mother was coming back.

Now that confidence was shaken, and I was dangerously close to completely losing it.

I needed to talk to someone who still believed. Someone who would agree with me that Rafe was giving up too soon, and that person clearly wasn't Charley.

I rode the subway uptown like a zombie. If anyone had been out to get me, this would have been the perfect opportunity. I was so out of it I almost missed my stop. And when I emerged, I saw that several messages had accumulated on my phone while I was underground.

All but one were from Charley, and I didn't want to hear anything she had to say. Patience's personal assistant had left a message, too, requesting that I go to my aunt's apartment for a meeting after school, but that barely registered.

I reached Prescott just as one period ended and before the next period started, so the hallways were filled with kids moving from class to class. There was enough buzzing around me to guess that the story of my brush with death had made the rounds. But I didn't pay any attention. I needed to find Natalie, so that she could remind me, in her crisp, logical way, about all of the things we knew that proved T.K. was alive.

It was our lunch period, and Natalie was at her usual table in the cafeteria, reading while she ate. "Hey," she said when I sat down beside her. "I heard what happened. Are you all right?"

And before I could answer, she told me about how she'd made Dr. Penske bring everyone in advanced physics outside to calculate how jumping the curb would affect a car's trajectory based on different velocities and rates of acceleration before and after the moment of impact. They'd proved with ninety-nine percent certainty that the driver must have accelerated after he jumped the curb and that he would've had to purposely turn the wheel to keep the car headed directly at me. Now they were focusing on analyzing some chips of black paint that the SUV might have deposited on the fire hydrant.

And it sounds bizarre, but her words were exactly what I needed. Listening to her explain in excruciating detail the measurements they'd taken and the calculations they'd done and the conclusions they'd drawn was more soothing than I ever would have thought listening to something like that could be.

Because as she talked, it was just like all of the other times we'd puzzled over the things we'd discovered, turning over pieces of evidence until we could decipher what they meant and where they fit in. And Natalie had seen all of the evidence I'd seen, and she knew everything I knew, and she'd put her scientist's stamp of approval on it all — well, maybe not Carolina, but the rest of it — and Natalie's stamp of approval was the next best thing to T.K.'s own stamp of approval.

Anyhow, as Natalie pulled out a piece of graph paper so she could diagram something for me, I felt the panic start to melt away and my confidence come flooding back.

Everything was going to be okay.

I just needed to figure out what I could do now that I no longer had Rafe's help.

■   ■   ■

I spent all of Modern Western Civilizations and precalc evaluating my options, and I was still trying to decide which one was best when I got to drama. My confusion from the previous day about what I'd say to Quinn was pretty much the furthest thing from my mind.

Once I saw him, though, it was hard not to notice how strangely he was acting. He sat next to me while the people who were up that day performed their scenes, and in the moments between scenes he asked all about how I was feeling and everything — but I felt like he was reading lines instead of actually talking to me, and he wasn't playing the part anywhere near as well as he played Romeo.

So, it was sort of a relief when class was over. But when he heard I was going to Patience's after school, he insisted on taking me there himself.

He hustled me through the hallways, out the door, and into a taxi with cool professionalism, like he was the Secret Service and I was the president, chatting the entire time about the performances we'd just seen. And since somehow that couldn't fill the three minutes it took to arrive at Patience's building, he started talking about the weather.

"How long do you think you'll be?" he asked as he paid the driver and walked me inside.

"I don't know. An hour, maybe?" I wasn't sure what Patience had in mind.

"Okay. I'll wait for you down here."

"You don't have to," I said. "I mean, I'd like to see you and everything, but if it's not convenient . . ."

"I promised Charley I'd take you home myself," he said. "She called me before."

"Oh," I said. Now I understood.

Quinn hadn't up and decided to do bodyguard duty on his own. He was here only out of a sense of obligation.

And whether his father was a bad guy or not, obligation wasn't exactly what I'd been hoping Quinn felt.

Thirty

Upstairs, the door was opened by a different uniformed maid than the one who'd served dinner the last time I had been there. She took me to Patience's study and told me that "Madame" would be with me shortly.

I'd still been plotting my next move, but now I was upset about Quinn, too, so I was sort of distracted. I heard the doorbell ring, but I didn't give it much thought.

Patience came in a few minutes later, and as usual she launched right into conversation. "You'll never guess who's in town and agreed to meet with us in person," she said. "I must say, I'm looking forward to giving him a piece of my mind."

"Who?" I said. Charley would have asked what piece, but I was just relieved that nobody had told Patience about my little accident.

And at that moment the maid ushered Thad into the room. "Here's Mr. Wilcox," the maid said to Patience. "Also, Mr. Babbitt's asked for a word with you. He's in the library."

"Hello, Mr. Wilcox," said Patience, shaking his hand. "Will you excuse me for a moment? I'll be right back." And she followed the maid out, leaving me alone with Thad.

The amazing thing was, he acted like nothing was wrong. He even tried to hug me in his own stiff, weaselish way, though I managed to slip out of his grasp.

"What do you think you're doing?" I demanded.

"What do you mean, Delia?" Thad asked calmly, settling himself in an armchair and crossing one leg over the other, taking care not to spoil the crease of his pants.

"What do I mean? Are you seriously asking me that?"

"Delia, you seem very emotional. Do you want me to get your aunt?"

"No, I want you to explain a few things to me. Like why you erased T.K.'s hard drive, for starters."

"Somebody tampered with your mother's computer?" he said, not blinking an eyelash. It was like he'd been taking lessons from Gwyneth.

"You were the only one who could've done it," I said. "What was on there that you didn't want anyone to see?"

He chuckled. "Your mother always said you had an active imagination, but I don't think she knew the half of it."

"What really brings you to town? Are you meeting with Trip Young and all of the other oil executives in his little club? Are you part of this whole plot?"

There was a subtle change in his expression, so slight that it was barely noticeable, but he stood up to face me. Which actually meant tower over me, since, like just about everyone else in the world, he was far taller than I'd ever be.

"Delia, I'm telling you this for your own good. You don't know what you're talking about, and if you're not careful, you're going to cause a lot of people a lot of trouble. Including yourself. So, if you're smart, you'll do what I say and stop nosing around in other people's business."

He managed to be condescending and menacing at the same time — and it was definitely the closest I'd ever seen him to having a personality. "Are you really threatening me?" I asked, astonished.

"Of course not," he said smoothly as my aunt's heels sounded in the corridor, signaling her return. "Ah, Ms. Truesdale-Babbitt, there you are. Shall we see if we can come to an agreement on those proposals I sent?" He returned to his armchair like I'd imagined everything he had just said to me.

There was no way I could sit there while they deliberated in legalese. Not when Rafe was coming back without my mother, and Charley wanted to regroup, and Quinn was acting like a watchdog instead of the guy who'd held my hand all through *Romeo and Juliet*. And now Thad had essentially confirmed everything I already knew and threatened me to boot.

It was all too much.

But I suddenly knew exactly what I needed to do.

■　　■　　■

I excused myself, and Patience and Thad were so busy with their documents that I didn't think they even noticed when I slipped out of the room and out of the apartment.

Downstairs, Quinn was playing cards with the doorman. "Oh, hey. That was quick," he said, folding his hand.

"Uh-huh," I said, brushing past him and out into the street. I didn't need him to do me any favors, not if the only reason he was doing them was because Charley was making him.

Quinn followed me out. "Delia, wait," he said.

"I can't talk right now. I have to be somewhere," I said, looking up and down Park Avenue for a cab.

"Where do you have to be?" Quinn asked.

"Chile," I said.

"Seriously, where are you going?"

"I told you," I said.

"You'll have better luck if you go over to Lexington at this time of day," said Quinn. "And since when do you take cabs?"

"I'm in a hurry," I said, heading down the block. "Besides, I don't know how to take the subway to the airport."

"You can't just go to Chile."

"Why not?"

"Because — because it's Chile."

I reached the corner and stuck my arm out into traffic.

"That's not how you do it," said Quinn. He put a thumb and finger to his lips and let out a piercing whistle, and a yellow cab swerved to a halt in front of us.

"Thanks." I ducked into the backseat.

"Move over," said Quinn.

"You're coming with me?" But I moved over and he shut the door. "Kennedy Airport, please," I told the driver while I checked my bag to make sure I had my passport and emergency credit card. Surely it would cover one plane ticket, and I'd be long gone before Patience ever saw the bill. Then I pulled out my phone, called information, and asked for the airline Rafe had taken to South America. I was in luck, for once — there was a direct flight to Santiago leaving in a couple of hours.

"Am I allowed to ask why you're in such a rush to get out of town?" Quinn asked after I'd finished making my reservation.

"Rafe suspended the investigation. So I need to pick up where he left off."

"Did he tell you why?"

I couldn't answer that without saying what I didn't want to say, but the question still made me think what I didn't want to think. That thick feeling was back in my throat. "It's not important why he stopped," I said. "He just stopped."

"And that's all you can tell me?"

I swallowed and nodded. The driver was taking us over the 59th Street Bridge, reversing the route the cab had taken that first night in New York. I stared hard out the window, trying to ward off a looming meltdown.

But I wasn't the one who melted down.

"WHAT IS WITH YOU?"

I flinched and even the cabdriver, who must see and hear all sorts of things every day, glanced back at us in the rearview mirror. I wondered if he knew the cabdriver Charley and I'd had the previous night.

"Wh-what do you mean?" I asked.

"You're the first girl I've met around here who's real, and who cares about things and likes to do things. But half the time, you decide the conversation's over in mid-sentence and take off. Or you ignore me when we're at school and other people are around, and you tell your cousin that there's nothing going on between us and that you're not interested in me at all."

"Me? What about you?" I demanded.

"What about me?"

"You're the master of saying one word and disappearing. And you have all these things that you care about, like Bea and Oliver and surfing and acting, but most people would never know that. Your father thinks you can't wait to be a banker and all your friends think you don't care about anything. And meanwhile you've gone from being a person who acted like he cared about me to a professional bodyguard doing a favor for my aunt. I mean, what is the whole Secret Service act about?"

His jaw was clenched. "I don't want anything to happen to you."

"Nothing's happened to me."

"Oh, like when you got hit by a car?"

"It didn't hit me."

"But I should have been there. I got caught up, talking to Mr. Dudley, and I was late, and I let you stand out there all alone."

"Quinn, that makes no sense."

"I just don't want it to happen again."

"What don't you want to happen?"

"I don't want anyone I care about to get hurt on my watch."

That shut us both up. We were silent for a while, each looking out our respective windows as we sped along the highway. And then I figured it out.

"This is about your mom, isn't it?"

He didn't reply right away. He just sort of shrugged. And then he said, "Probably."

I moved closer and leaned into him. After a moment, he put his arm around my shoulder.

And we just stayed like that, not talking, the rest of the way to the airport.

Thirty-one

It was a good thing that Quinn had insisted on coming with me, because I didn't have any cash and the credit card machine was broken, so I needed him to pay the cab fare. I also tried to convince him to take the cab home, but he insisted on following me into the terminal. It was nice to have him there, even if he did keep trying to change my mind.

"Are you sure you want to do this?" he asked yet again as we took our places at the end of a very long check-in line.

"I have to," I said. "Nobody else is doing anything, so I need to do what I can."

"Are you sure you can't wait until Rafe gets back, so he can tell us what he knows?"

I was scared of what Rafe might know, but Quinn didn't know that. "I'm sick of waiting," I said. "In fact, I'm done with waiting. And I can always call and ask Rafe when I get there."

"You'll ask me what when you get where?" somebody asked from behind me.

I spun around. In his jeans and T-shirt, and without a tie

with cute animals on it, I almost didn't recognize him. But it was Rafe. He had the rumpled, tired look of someone who'd been traveling for days, though his smile was as kind as ever. I only hoped it wasn't because he was gearing up to tell me things I didn't want to hear.

"What are you doing here?" I asked.

"My flight just arrived. And I saw you and your friend from the escalator when I was on my way to the baggage claim. So I thought I'd come say hello. Where are you off to?"

"Yes, Delia, where are you off to?" asked somebody else from behind me. And I didn't have to spin around this time, because Charley has a very distinctive voice.

It was like a convention. All we needed now was Patience and the Monkeys.

"I told you — she's going to Chile," Quinn said to Charley. He turned to me with a sheepish look. "I might have texted Charley while you were making your flight reservation."

"So you're the aunt," said Rafe, taking Charley's hand in his. "Rafael Francisco Valenzuela Sáenz de Santamaría, at your service. It's a delight to meet you in person. Now I can see where Delia gets her beauty, as well as her charm."

I thought that was laying it on pretty thick, but Charley didn't seem to mind. With an effort, she pulled her gaze away from Rafe and back to me. "You're going to Chile?" she said.

"Yes," I said.

"To Chile," she repeated.

"Uh-huh," I said. "It's a country. In South America. Maybe you've heard of it?"

And then it was just like that first night on the roof. But instead of Dieter cracking up, Charley cracked up.

"You're laughing at me?" I asked, incredulous. "After all of this, after everything I've been through, and the way you sold me out — you're laughing at me."

"Your aunt is just appreciating the irony of the situation," said Rafe. "Isn't that so?"

Charley only nodded, her lips pressed tightly together. I could tell it was taking every ounce of restraint she had not to crack up all over again.

I couldn't help what happened next. And it was her own fault. I mean, she was *laughing* at me.

"What irony?" I demanded. "What's so funny about wanting to go rescue my mother? Just because everyone else is giving up doesn't mean I'm giving up. And there's no reason to give up, because T.K.'s alive, and the only reason to give up would be if you knew that she wasn't, but she is —"

"Delia!" Charley tried to interrupt me.

"— even if you don't think so and you made Rafe come back and even if Rafe doesn't think so, which is why he agreed to come back —"

"Delia!" Charley said again.

"— but that wouldn't make sense because she tried to call me and Carolina saw her — only in her head, but she saw her —"

"Rafe," Charley said. "Please tell me you have it with you."

Rafe was rummaging in his coat pockets. "Where did I put it?"

"— and there were rumors about someone who fit her description in Patagonia —"

"Ah," said Rafe, pulling out his phone.

"Show her already," urged Charley.

"— and the *Polar Star* didn't really disappear, somebody just made it look like it did —"

Rafe stuck his phone in front of my face. There, on the screen, was a photo of a little boy in overalls, holding a toy dump truck.

"So?" I said.

"Look at the picture," he said.

"I am," I said.

He leaned in to peer at the screen. "Oh. Wrong one. That's my nephew, Lorenzo. Adorable, isn't he?"

"Rafe," said Charley impatiently.

Rafe took his phone back and fiddled with it. "Here we go," he said, handing it to me.

This time it was a photo of Rafe, wearing the same clothes he had on now, like the picture had just been taken that morning, eight days after I'd first met Carolina Carderas.

And standing next to Rafe, smiling into the camera, was my mother.

Thirty-two

I ended up not going to Chile. I was also sort of glad to leave the airport, because I couldn't even begin to imagine what all of the people who'd witnessed our little scene must have been thinking.

Rafe wasn't comfortable explaining everything there, in such a public place, so we decided to go back to the loft. Quinn was going to come with us, but Charley put a gentle hand on his arm.

"I owe you — yet again," she said. "But we need to discuss this with Delia alone. Do you mind?"

"That's all right," he said. "I understand." He turned to me. "Call me later?"

"Yes."

"Promise?"

"I promise," I said.

And then he leaned down and kissed me. And this time it wasn't Romeo kissing Juliet. It was Quinn kissing Delia. And that was even better.

■　　■　　■

Rafe wouldn't even talk in front of the cabdriver. At least, not about my mother or Chile or anything interesting. He was fine with talking to Charley about Charley, and laughing at everything she said like she was some sort of brilliant comic genius. But it wasn't until we were behind closed doors at Charley's that he started answering my questions.

"Your mother's safe in Chile, but she doesn't want anyone to know that, obviously. So you must be very careful not to say anything to anybody at all," he told me.

"Were we right, though?" I asked. "Was it the people at EAROFO? Or Navitaco? Or Thad?"

"Yes," said Rafe.

"Yes? Which one are you saying yes to?"

"All of them. But in different ways."

"What about Hunter Riley?" I asked, even though I wasn't sure I wanted to know the answer.

"That's complicated," said Rafe.

"Could you be any more cryptic?" I asked in frustration.

He smiled. "Possibly."

"Who's hungry?" said Charley.

"You're changing the subject," I said.

"No, I'm starving, and you probably are, too. And we have a long night of planning ahead of us, and there's no way I can do that on an empty stomach. I'm thinking tacos. What do you think?"

Suddenly, I was ravenous. "Lots of tacos," I said. "And how's our ice cream supply?"

"I'll go out and pick up provisions," said Charley. "Rafe, do you like tacos?"

"I adore tacos. But why don't I go with you? I can help you carry everything."

"Sure," said Charley. She was looking at Rafe like she'd never looked at Lars or Midwest Bill. I hoped he enjoys teen movie classics.

So they went to pick up dinner, and I changed out of my uniform and into a pair of jeans. Then I took the phone and a cushion from the sofa, climbed up on the wide ledge in front of the window, and made myself comfortable. The sun had just set, and the sky was a bluish purple over the skyline.

A flash of movement on the sidewalk below caught my eye, and I glanced down, wondering if it was Charley and Rafe, already back from the taco place. But as I pressed my face against the window, I saw a figure step into a shadowed doorway across the street. I waited a moment, but nobody stepped back out. It must have been someone who lived there, I decided, going into the building. None of the lights went on in the upper floors, but that didn't necessarily mean anything. Anyhow, I had more important things to do than spy on my neighbors. Like phoning Quinn.

He answered on the first ring. "Hey, Juliet," he said. "You

called." In the background, I could hear Bea and Oliver chattering and what sounded like a cartoon on the TV.

"I told you I would," I said.

"Did Rafe tell you the whole story?"

"Only a bit. He's supposed to tell me more later."

"And then you'll tell me?"

"Definitely," I said.

"Like maybe tomorrow night?"

"I could do that," I said, wondering if he could tell from my voice that the uncontrollable smile thing was happening all over again.

"I could do that, too," he said.

"Then I'll plan on it."

There was a crash behind him, and one of the kids squealed. "I'm babysitting," said Quinn. "And I'd better run before they destroy the place. But I'll see you tomorrow?"

"See you tomorrow," I said.

I sat there in the window for a while after we hung up, the uncontrollable smile still on my face, watching as the bluish purple of the sky slowly darkened to black. It had been a long time since I'd felt this way, like everything was right with the world. Or almost right.

I mean, it was wonderful to know for a fact that T.K. was okay. But in a way, everything was just beginning. After all, we still had to figure out how she could get her life back without having to worry about anyone taking it away again. Otherwise she wouldn't be able to come home. And based on what little Rafe had told me, this would be a seriously difficult knot to untangle.

So, I had a lot to take care of.

But for now I was just going to think about seeing the photo of Rafe and T.K., and kissing Quinn. And then maybe some more about kissing Quinn.

To be continued . . .